GOOD 2 GO

THE TEFLON QUEEN 5

DEEP COVER

A NOVEL

SILK WHITE

Good 2 Go Publishing

ISBN: 9781943686773
Copyright ©2015
Published 2015 by Good2Go Publishing
7311 W. Glass Lane • Laveen, AZ 85339
www.good2gopublishing.com
twitter @good2gobooks
G2G@good2gopublishing.com
Facebook.com/good2gopublishing
ThirdLane Marketing: Brian James
Brian@good2gopublishing.com
Cover design: Davida Baldwin
Interior Layout: Mychea, Inc

Printed in the U.S.A.

BOOKS BY THIS AUTHOR

10 Secrets to Publishing Success
Business Is Business
Business Is Business 2
Married To Da Streets
Never Be The Same
Stranded
Sweet Pea's Tough Choices
Tears of a Hustler
Tears of a Hustler 2
Tears of a Hustler 3
Tears of a Hustler 4
Tears of a Hustler 5
Tears of a Hustler 6
Teflon Queen
Teflon Queen 2
Teflon Queen 3
Teflon Queen 4
Teflon Queen 5
The Serial Cheater
Time Is Money (An Anthony Stone Novel)
48 Hours to Die (An Anthony Stone Novel)

WEB SERIES
The Hand I Was Dealt
Episodes 1-8 Now Available Free On You Tube

Acknowledgements

To all of you who are reading this, thank you for stepping inside the bookstore, stopping by the library, or downloading a copy of The Teflon Queen 5. I hope you have enjoyed this read from top to bottom. My goal is to get better and better with each story. I want to thank everyone for all their love and support. It is definitely appreciated! Now without further ado Ladies and Gentleman, I give you *The Teflon Queen 5*.

$ilk White

THE TEFLON QUEEN 5

DEEP COVER

PROLOGUE

Angela and, Ashley stepped off the private jet and hopped into the SUV that awaited their arrival. They had just arrived in London. But they weren't there on vacation or to site see, they were there on business.

"Okay, Troy talk to me. We didn't have time to get briefed on the jet for this mission so you're going to have to fill us in," Angela said as she and, Ashley checked the magazines on their handguns.

"I would have loved to make the trip with you ladies but the captain had other plans for me," Troy said as the trio communicated through their earpieces. "Well it seems like several of our country's best agents has been coming up dead. Twelve in the last two months."

"Where were these agents last seen?" Ashley asked with a concerned look on her face.

"A few of them were sent to go capture a man that goes by the name, the Lion. Needless to say all the agents never returned or was ever heard from again," Troy paused for a second. "The other agents were all murdered in their homes along with their families."

"Sounds fishy if you ask me," Angela said. She knew it wasn't easy to kill a trained agent. You had to have some serious skills to pull something like that off. "So what are we doing in London?"

"One of the missing agents popped up in a hospital in London when he gave them his name it popped up in our data base. You and Ashley need to get as much information out of the agent as possible we need to know what he knows about, the Lion and if he has any info on any of the other missing agents."

"Copy," Angela said as the SUV pulled up in front of the hospital, and from the looks of it, the place was packed. Angela and Ashley entered the hospital with serious looks on their faces. Twelve agents gone missing and presumed dead wasn't something they took lightly. "What room?"

"704," Troy's voice crackled through Angela's earpiece. Angela and Ashley stepped on the elevator and pressed seven. The doors to the elevator closed and the elevator carried them up to the seventh floor. Angela and Ashley stepped off the elevator and immediately saw several nurses running down the hall in a panic they looked up and saw the number 704 above the door. Angela ran to the room and looked inside. Laying in the bed was a man with both of his legs missing and a large bandage wrapped around his head. The monitor above the agents head held a loud steady beep pronouncing him dead. Angela grabbed the nurse closes to her by the arm. "What happened?"

"I...I don't know," the nurse said nervously. "I just checked on him ten minutes ago and he was fine."

"I saw a tall man and a short Asian woman exit this room just as the monitor went off," another nurse volunteered.

"Do you remember what they were wearing?" Ashley asked.

"Yes they were both wearing black trench coats," the nurse informed.

Angela and Ashley quickly exited the room to look for the couple in matching black trench coats. "Troy I need you to be my eyes we're looking for a tall male and a short Asian female both wearing black trench coats."

Troy pressed a few keys on his computer and hacked into the hospital's security cameras. "Found them. They're on the elevator heading down to the lobby."

Angela and Ashley took off in a sprint towards the staircase. They ran down the stairs skipping two at a time until they finally reached the lobby. Angela stepped out of the staircase and walked at a normal pace. "Okay Troy, where are they?"

"Straight ahead. You can't miss them," Troy replied. "Be careful I doubt they're wearing trench coats for a fashion statement."

"Copy," Angela said as she looked over at Ashley. "I'll take the tall man and you take the chick."

"Why do you get to have all the fun?" Ashley protested. "I want tall man."

"Fine I'll take the chick," Angela said as the woman in the trench coat looked back and made eye contact with her. "I think she just made me so get ready to move."

***

"I think we have company," the woman in the trench coat said to her partner.

"You sure about that Roxy?" The tall man asked.

"Positive," Roxy said looking for the quickest exit. "We split up. Move on my que,"

"Copy," tall man said as he reached in his trench coat and grabbed the handle of his machine gun. Roxy took a couple of more steps before she flung her trench coat off and spun around holding a machine gun with an banana clip hanging from the base. She squeezed down on the trigger and swayed her arms from side to side killing any and everybody in her line of fire.

"Get down!" Angela yelled as she dived behind a wall. Ashely quickly dashed inside the room closest to her as bullets decorated the wall just above her head.

Roxy turned and took off in a sprint towards the exit, when out of nowhere, one of the hospital police officers roughly tackled her down to the floor. Roxy hit the floor and bounced backed up to her feet before the officer could count to two. The officer threw a wild right hook with bad intentions Roxy caught the officers arm in mid swing, landed a vicious elbow to the man's rib cage, raised her elbow, and broke the officers arm, then finished him off with a violent hip toss down to the hard floor. Another officer ran up, but Roxy quickly removed her back up 9mm from the small of her back and put a bullet right between the officer's eyes, in a rapid succession, she put down three other officers with pinpoint accuracy who called themselves trying to be heroes. Roxy sprang back up to her feet when she was tackled from behind. Angela tackled Roxy from behind and the two went sliding across the floor. Angela went to apply a chokehold on the female assassin, but before Angela could lock her arm under Roxy's throat, she somehow squirmed out of Angela's grip. Angela punched Roxy in her face then rushed her back into the wall. As soon as Roxy's back hit the wall, she dipped up under

Angela's next punch and landed three quick blows of her own. The punches snapped Angela's head back and stunned her the punches came so fast that Angela could only use her face to block the punches. Before Angela could recover from the blows, Roxy ran and charged Angela. She hit her hard lifting her slightly off her feet as the two went crashing through the glass door that said emergency only on it. Roxy made it up first but Angela quickly swept her feet from under her sending her crashing violently down on a pile of broken glass. Angela mounted Roxy, and landed a few punches to her face. Just as Angela was about to go in for the kill a police officer tackled her off top of Roxy from behind. The officer had no clue what was going on all he knew was that shots had been fired and he was trying to gain control of the situation. Angela flipped the officer off her, grabbed him by his shoulders and jammed her knee in the pit of his stomach., Then she landed a sharp elbow down into the officers back she then pulled her Five-Seven pistol from her holster and aimed it at the fleeing assassin but she couldn't take the shot because there were too many innocent people in her line of fire. "Shit!" Angela cursed as she took off after the Asian assassin.

***

Ashley sprinted down the hall, chasing after Tall Man. She had a decent shot but wanted to get closer. If possible, she wanted to take the Tall Man alive and see if she could maybe get some information out of him. Tall Man reached the end of the hall way and opened fire on the staff as well as a few police officers trying to get In his way.

"Hey!" Ashley yelled. When Tall Man turned around Ashley fired four shots into his chest dropping him instantly. Ashley eased towards tall man's body, once she was close enough she kicked his machine gun out of arms reach at the same time Tall Man raised his leg and kicked Ashley in the chest sending her sliding across the floor. The impact from the kick was so powerful that it caused Ashley to lose possession of her gun. Ashley quickly sprang back to her feet as Tall Man closed in on her. Tall Man threw a powerful jab that if connected would of more than likely broken Ashley's face. Ashley slipped the jab and delivered a hard knee to Tall Man's stomach, followed by a hard elbow to Tall Man's temple. Ashley landed several hard blows to Tall Man's face but the blows didn't seem to faze him. Tall Man grabbed a hand full of Ashley's hair and slammed her head violently into the wall. Ashley ducked the next punch, pulled a sharp knife from her utility belt, and sliced Tall Man's arm. Ashley followed up and sliced Tall Man across his chest and his thigh before he even realized what was going on.

Tall Man looked down at his blood and flashed a smile. He quickly reached behind his back and produced a small handgun; he raised his arm and fired off a shot.

When Ashley saw Tall Man, reach she did an army roll, came up, and tossed the knife in his direction. She looked on and watched as the knife flipped through the air before finding a home in the tall man's throat. Tall Man tried to remove the knife from his throat but it was no use blood gushed out of the wound and quickly covered his fingers. After a few seconds Tall Man finally collapsed down to the floor and took his last breath. "Tall Man is down where are you Angela?" Ashley yelled through her earpiece as she ran outside in hopes to catch up with Angela.

***

Roxy ran out into the street like a mad woman. Up ahead she saw man riding a motorcycle heading in her direction., Without thinking twice Roxy stuck out her arm and close-lined the rider off the bike. She ran and snatched the helmet off the man's head, then hopped on his bike, and burned rubber. Just as

Roxy pulled off she felt a bullet explode in the back of her bulletproof vest. The impact from the shot almost made her lose control of the bike but she somehow managed to keep control.

Angela ran out into the middle of the street and fired off a shot that hit the Asian assassin but she somehow maintained control of the bike. Angela quickly ran and stopped the first car she saw which happened to be a black Camaro. "I'm sorry sir but I need your car!" she said as she removed the man from his vehicle at gunpoint. Angela got behind the wheel and gunned the engine. There was no way she was letting the assassin get away. The Camaro zipped through the streets at a high speed Angela navigated the sports car as if it was a racecar. The engine revved loudly as the speedometer rose quickly.

Roxy weaved in and out of traffic like a mad woman. She quickly bunny hopped onto the curb and rode on the sidewalk forcing pedestrians to damn near kill themselves trying to get out the way of the mad rider. Roxy hit the corner hard leaning herself along with the bike so low to the ground that her knee threatened to scrape the ground. Up ahead, Roxy noticed a busy intersection. Without thinking twice she sped up and ran through the intersection barely avoiding several near death collisions. Behind her, several cars slammed into one another causing a semi roadblock. Roxy then took that opportunity to hop on the freeway.

"Shit!" Angela cursed as she swerved around several damaged vehicles barely avoiding a few collisions herself. Car horns blared loudly as people got out of their vehicles yelling and screaming. Angela cut the wheel hard to the right and merged onto the freeway. The Camaro's engine roared as it picked up speed. Angela kept her eyes on her target the Asian assassin was only four car lengths in front of her.

Roxy looked over her shoulder and saw the

black Camaro speeding up on her left side. She quickly swerved and weaved from lane to lane, her hair that hung out the back of her helmet flew wildly all over the place as she reached speeds well over 100mph.

Roxy glanced over her shoulder again and noticed that the Camaro was still keeping up. She then quickly removed her 9mm from her thigh holster, aimed behind her, and fired four shots into the Camaro's windshield.

Angela quickly ducked her head down as several bullets shattered her windshield. Angela held the steering wheel steady with one hand, grabbed her Five-Seven pistol with the other hand, and stuck it out the window. Angela sent several shot in the Asian assassin's direction.

Roxy weaved from out of one lane to the next when a bullet hit her back tire causing her to lose control of the bike. "Argggghhh!" she yelped as her body was thrown from the bike. Roxy's body landed violently on the unforgiving freeway. When Roxy hit the ground, her momentum from the crash caused her body to roll across the concrete for at least fifteen seconds before finally coming to a stop. Roxy quickly peeled herself up from off the ground and took off in a sprint., She ran with a slight limp and wasn't able to reach her maximum speed due to the crash. During the crash, Roxy loss possession of her pistol and was now weapon less. She ran over towards the ledge of the bridge, took a deep breath then swan dived off the bridge down into the water below.

Angela pulled the Camaro up to the ledge and hopped out. She ran over towards the ledge, looked down into the water, and didn't see anything. Angela kicked off her boots and climbed up on the ledge.

"I know you're not thinking about jumping down in that water!" Troy's voice crackled through Angela's earpiece. "Angela think about this."

"No time to think!" Angela said as she drove off the ledge down into the water. The coldness of the water shocked Angela's body at first but she knew in a few seconds her body would get used to the frigid cold. Angela swam under water blindly. With the water being so dirty, it made it hard for her to see clearly. As Angela swam, she spotted movement out the corner of her eye she looked over to her left and saw a pair of legs enter some sort of underwater cave. Angela swam over toward the cave and just as she arrived, the Asian assassin slammed the steel-checkered door shut and turned it lock. Angela tried her best to get the door open but it was no use.

Roxy and Angela stared off long and hard at one another before Roxy finally swam away leaving Angela there on the outside looking in.

Angela hit the door out of frustration, as she had no other choice but to swim back up to the surface.

ONE

WHAT THE HELL IS GOING ON?

Angela reached headquarters and knew something was wrong from how everyone was looking at her. She grabbed a cup of coffee and headed down the hall but stopped dead in her tracks when she heard Captain Spiller stick his head out of the conference room and call her name.

"Glad you could finally join us. We need you in this meeting with us," Captain Spiller said as he escorted Angela inside the conference room. Angela stepped inside the room and immediately saw Ashley Troy, and another blonde hair woman she had never seen before Angela helped herself to a seat. "Okay what did I miss?"

"This here is lieutenant Mary Wiggings. She's head of a secret group called the TSA (Tactical Secret Agents) and she's here to shine some light on the twelve missing agents," Captain Spiller explained.

"Thank you captain," Mary stood to her feet. "The TSA had one mission and that was to find and eliminate the world's most dangerous terrorist, a man that goes by the name, the Lion. I sent several agents out to eliminate, the Lion and none of them made it back alive, the Lion has even taken things a step further and had the families of the agents murdered in cold blood. I've heard rumors that, the Lion is scheduled to be in Dubai sometime this week He's been off the grid for a while so if he's popping up now something big must be about to go down," Mary paused. "Here's where the story gets tricky my best field agent Matt Hardy seems to have switched side on us and now he's working for, the Lion."

"Wait; so you mean to tell me that your best agent is a traitor?" Angela asked with a confused look on her face.

"Yes and I believe agent Hardy helped, the Lion take out the other twelve agents I sent to eliminate the terrorist now agent Matt Hardy is missing," Mary replied. "Angela you sat down with a sketch artist the other day am I correct?"

Angela nodded her head. "Correct."

"Well here's a picture of the Asia assassin," Mary pulled the assassins picture up on the big projector screen. "Her name is Roxy Young. She's a former Asian agent highly skilled and trained, she's wanted in several countries and is said to be, the Lion's best soldier," Mary clicked a button on the remote she held and the screen went from the picture of Roxy to a picture of Roxy at an airport. "This is a picture of Roxy arriving at the airport in, Dubai yesterday," Mary clicked a button on the remote and this time a picture of Matt Hardy standing in an airport appeared on the projector. "Here's a picture of agent Matt Hardy arriving at the airport in, Dubai this morning, now I have no clue on what, the Lion is up too but what I do know is that it's going down in Dubai and it's going down soon."

"So what do you want us to do?" Ashley asked speaking for the first time.

"Well I was told that you all were the best agents available."

"No we're the best agent's period," Ashley corrected her.

"Didn't mean to offend anyone," Mary apologized. "What I need is for you and your team is to go to, Dubai and stop whatever, the Lion and his team has planned, that is the mission if you choose to accept."

"We accept," Angela said quickly. Even though they would be heading out to, Dubai blindly, Angela looked forward to seeing her good friend Roxy again.

"Well, Dubai here we come," Troy said in a sarcastic tone.

TWO

WELCOME TO DUBAI

Angela sat on the jet, reading agent Matt Hardy's file. She was having a hard time trying to figure out why he would trade sides when he was one of the best agents to ever lace em up. "I want everyone to be on point tonight this Matt Hardy guy is well trained and supposed to be as dangerous as they come."

"Something real big is about to go down, I can feel it." Ashley chimed in.

"Yup and I have a strange feeling that we're going to be smack dead in the middle of it." Troy said sarcastically. "I think I found something," Troy said pointing to the screen on his laptop. "It says that the mayor is supposed to be having a big nonprofit event tonight at some big fancy hotel. I'm willing to bet my last dollar that's where we'll find Matt Hardy and Roxy."

"Now all we have to do is figure out a way to get in there," Ashley said.

"I have an idea." Angela said with a wicked smile on her face.

***

The trio entered their hotel room, put down their gear, and got straight to work.

"So what's your big idea?" Ashley asked.

"We kidnap the mayor's daughter and I go to the event and impersonate her and see what I can find out." Angela suggested. She knew it was a dangerous idea but at the moment, it was looking like their best option. Troy pulled up a picture of the mayor's daughter, pulled out a machine, clicked a few buttons on his computer, and watched as the machine began making an amazing lifelike mask that looked just like the mayor's daughter. "Her name in Kimberly Hernandez."

"You have an address for her?" Ashley asked.

THREE

KIMBERLY HERNANDEZ

"Come on, I have to go or else I'm going to be late," Kimberly said to Mike, her personal bodyguard who was paid to follow her around everywhere she went. Kimberly had been out shopping all day and had a slight attitude because the last store she went into didn't have her size in the dress that she wanted.

"Calm down, I'm sure we'll find the dress at the next store." Mike said.

"I don't even want to go to this stupid event tonight. I'm only going because my father is making me," Kimberly huffed as they entered the next store. Immediately Kimberly spotted the perfect dress. "I want to try that one on," she told the salesman. Kimberly got the dress then hurried into the dressing room. Mike stood right next to the dressing room door when he saw a woman enter the store wearing a blonde wig and a pair of dark sunglasses. Mike saw the woman pull something out of her purse. He went for his gun, but it was too late.

Ashley stepped in the store, spotted, Kim's bodyguard and took him down quickly. Ashley pulled her tranquilizer gun from her purse and shot Mike in his neck. She then turned her gun on salesman and put him down. Ashley then quickly climbed over the counter and removed the security camera.

Kimberly stepped out of the dressing room looking like a princess with her expensive dress on.

"What do you think?" She looked up and saw a woman in dark shades aiming a gun her. Kimberly quickly threw her hands up in the air. "Don't shoot."

"Night, night." Ashley said as she fired a shot into Kimberly's neck. Once everyone was down Troy entered the store and helped get Kimberly and Mike's body in the back of the limousine.

FOUR

DO WHAT YOU GOTTA DO

Matt Hardy stepped out the limousine dressed in a nice black tuxedo. He stood six foot even, his blue eyes, thin mustache, and muscular frame were only a few of his eye-catching features that kept all the ladies flocking in his direction. Matt Hardy entered the hotel and spotted nothing but the rich and wealthy. "I'm in," he said through his earpiece.

"Okay, stick to the plan and make sure you

remain unseen until the mayor and his daughter arrive," Roxy replied. Roxy walked throughout the ballroom wearing a long plain black gown that dragged across the floor. She looked like an innocent young lady but the truth was she was one of the most violent people in the entire building. Roxy grabbed a glass of champagne off one of the waiter's trays and sipped it slowly as she took note of her surroundings. Across the room she spotted Matt Hardy, he was a very handsome man but Roxy didn't trust him. It was just something about him that she couldn't put her finger on. As Roxy was watching Matt Hardy, a man in an all-white tuxedo with hair that rested on his shoulders bumped into her causing her to spill her drink.

"Excuse ma'am I'm sorry about that," the man said politely. "Can I get you another drink?"

"No that won't be necessary," Roxy replied with a smile.

"Well it was good seeing," the man said as he

walked by and slipped a small piece of paper in Roxy's hand and kept on walking. Roxy held on to the paper and quickly disappeared inside the ladies room. She checked each and every stall making sure it was empty before she unfolded the note and began to read it.

"Keep an eye on Matt Hardy I don't trust him make sure he pulls off his part of the mission and make sure you take the mayor's daughter out...head shot!.......From yours truly, the Lion"

When she was done reading the note, Roxy quickly ripped it into tiny pieces then flushed it down the toilet. Just as she was about to exit the ladies room, she heard Matt Hardy's voice crackle through her earpiece.

"The mayor and his daughter just arrived."

FIVE

I DON'T TRUST YOU

Angela stepped out the limousine dressed in a nice expensive silver gown. The life-like mask she wore worked perfectly not even the mayor could tell the difference between his daughter and the fake.

"Are you okay tonight honey?" the mayor asked looking down at Kimberly.

"Yes I'm fine. I'm going to go to the ladies room I'll be right back," Kimberly said. Once she was away from her father, she spoke into her earpiece. "Hey Troy talk to me."

Troy sat in the back of his van that was parked three blocks away from the hotel. "I'm tapped into all the security cameras now and I've just spotted Matt Hardy."

"I'll go after him."

"No Angela we need you to stay close to the mayor We're not sure why, Matt Hardy is here but I'm sure it has something to do with the mayor," Troy said. "Ashley you'll have to go after Matt Hardy."

"Copy," Ashley replied as she grabbed a glass of champagne off one of the moving trays and downed the bubbly liquid in one gulp. "Where is he?"

"Turn to your right and you can't miss him." Troy's voice echoed through, Ashley's earpiece.

***

Matt Hardy stood in the middle of the floor

pretending to sip from his glass of champagne. He held the glass up to his lips while his eyes scanned the entire room. On first glance, he spotted an attractive woman out the corner of his eye that seemed to be discreetly watching him. Matt Hardy didn't know who she was but from her muscular shoulders and toned legs, he knew that she wasn't just some ordinary woman in an expensive gown who ever this lady was she was here for a reason. Matt had been trained to spot things that stuck out on people. He was also trained to kill. "Room 540 there's a briefcase inside I need you to go get it and be carefully there will be armed men guarding the room. Roxy's voice snapped through, Matt's earpiece. "My job was to kill the mayor's daughter. Why the change of plan?" Matt asked as he sat his drink down and headed over towards the elevators.

"Stop asking so many questions. You have ten minutes to get that briefcase before another crew of armed guards come to get the case so you better move fast," Roxy told him.

"Shit!" Matt Hardy cursed under his breath he didn't know what, the Lion was up to but whatever it was it was bound to be trouble. Matt stepped on the elevator and pressed five. Just as the doors were closing he noticed the woman with the toned legs heading towards the elevators as well. Matt Hardy stood on the elevator, quickly removed his Berta from his holster, and screwed a silencer onto the barrel, the entire time he made sure he kept his head down so the security camera couldn't catch his identity. The elevator doors open and, Matt stepped off with a two handed grip on his weapon he turned the corner and spotted three men with suits and earpieces guarding room 540.

"Sir no one is allowed down here. I'm going to have to ask you..."the first man said, right before his head exploded.

Psst!

Matt quickly fired a shot that hit the next guard

in the neck; he didn't even wait for the guard's body to hit the floor before he moved on to the last guard. The last guard's eyes lit up in fear he went to reach for his weapon but frozen when he felt the barrel of the hot silencer pressed into the middle of his forehead.

"What's in the briefcase?" Matt growled into the remaining guard's ear.

"I don't know man I don't ask questions I just do what I'm told," the guard replied with a scared look on his face. A few seconds ago, he was cool now he was a sweaty mess. Matt reached down into the guard's pocket and took his room key. In a swift motion, he swung his gun with his entire might and knocked the last guard out cold. Matt Hardy quickly entered room 540, and then looked down at his watch. He would have to move quick being as though he only had five minutes left to retrieve the briefcase and get out of the room undetected. Matt eased his way inside the room with a tight two-handed grip on his weapon; he inched his way further inside the room when out of nowhere he was roughly grabbed in a bear hug from behind then violently slammed through a glass coffee table that rested in the middle of the room. During the fall, Matt lost possession of his gun. He looked up and saw a big strong man standing over him with a no nonsense look on his face. The big man roughly snatched, Matt to his feet and threw him violently against the wall. Matt bounced off the wall and landed a three-punch combination to the big man's chin. He then quickly followed up with a sharp kick to the side of the big man's leg. The kick didn't faze the big man as he ducked low and came up with an uppercut that was intended to take, Matt's head. Matt quickly weaved the punch and delivered a sharp elbow that bounced off the side of the big man's head. Before the big man could figure out what was going on his legs were swept from up under him and he went down hard. Matt raised his leg and stomped the big man's head into the floor breaking his nose in the process. The big man quickly hopped back up to his feet with blood running down his face, he tasted some of his blood and smiled. "Yeah motherfucker this the type of shit I like!" the big man said as he removed a hunting knife from the small of his back and held it in a firm grip. Matt Hardy took his fighting stance as the big man inched closer and closer.

***

Ashley stepped on the elevator with a fake smile on her face. "What floor?"

"He went to the fifth floor," Troy answered. "Please be careful. From the looks of it there's a lot going on up there."

"Copy," Ashely replied. When the elevator doors opened, immediately, Ashley could hear a loud commotion coming from down the hall and around the corner. Ashely quickly removed her .380 from her purse and screwed the silencer on the barrel as she reached room 540. Outside of the room, she spotted two bodies sprawled out across the carpeted floor she quickly stepped over the bodies and entered the room.

SIX

NOT ON MY WATCH

Angela walked through the ballroom shaking people's hand who she had never seen before in her life the mask she wore was doing wonders. Angela smiled and laughed with the entire stranger while the entire time, Troy was giving her updates in her ear.

"There's something going down on the fifth floor upstairs, Ashley just made it up there."

"Is Matt Hardy up there?" Angela asked.

"Yes he is," Troy answered quickly.

"Keep me posted," Angela said as she noticed the mayor walking up to her.

"Hey, Kim I have someone I want you to meet he's a good friend of mines," the mayor said with a smile. "This here is my friend, Leo and this is my daughter Kimberly," the mayor introduced the two.

"Nice to meet you Leo," Angela said as she shook the man's hand.

"The pleasure is all mines," Leo said as bent down and kissed the back of, Angela's hand. "You smell very unique."

"Thank you."

"Hey don't be trying to push up on my daughter right in front of me," the mayor said in a joking manner as he playfully nudged, Leo with his elbow. "I have to keep my eye on you," The mayor laughed. "Leo must be short for Lion the way you hunting my daughter down."

Just the word, Lion caused Angela's head to

snap in Leo's direction she didn't mean to be so obvious but she couldn't help herself. "Stop embarrassing me dad," Angela tried to clean it up, she then turned her focus back on, Leo. "Besides I would like to know a little more about, the Lion," she smiled.

"Well, I'll leave you two alone I have a few more other guest I need to greet," the mayor said as he left, Kimberly and, Leo alone to talk.

"So, Lion I mean Leo tell me a little bit about yourself," Angela chuckled. The Lion smiled as he reached out and stuck Angela with something then turned and walked off.

"Ouch! He just stuck me with something," Angela said as she began to follow, the Lion. "I have eyes on, the Lion he's heading for the exit now."

"What did he stick you with?" Troy asked.

"I don't know," Angela replied as her vision became blurry and she could no longer walk straight. "I'm going after him."

"No, Angela you can't you have to get back to the van so we can figure out what was injected into you."

"I can't let him get away, Troy. I saw his face," Angela said as she stumbled through the crowd.

"Are you okay sweetie?" one of the mayor's friends asked as he noticed, Kimberly walking like she wasn't coherent.

"Yes I'm fine I just need some air," Angel said as she exited the hotel and looked around. "I can't see. Where is he?"

"I'm looking now," Troy said looking at his computer screen. After looking at his monitor for a few seconds, Troy spotted a man in a white tuxedo get in an space gray Jaguar. "To your left he just got inside of a gray Jaguar."

Angela stumbled towards the valet attendant as she saw a blurred gray car pass her. She walked over to an older woman that was exiting her vehicle, quickly slipped behind the wheel, and pulled recklessly out into traffic.

"I don't think this is a good idea," Troy's voice echoed through Angela's earpiece. Angela ignored Troy's advice as she sideswiped another car on the road.

"I need you to guide me Troy!" Angela yelled.

"Keep going straight through that intersection!" Troy replied. Angela stomped down on the gas pedal and zoomed through the intersection as she scraped up against two other vehicles in the process. "Now what?"

"He just ran through another intersection but hold on because the light is red!" Troy told her. Angela ignored, Troy and picked up speed there was no way she was going to let, the Lion out of her site he was the biggest terrorist that America had seen in the last decade not to mention the most violent. Angela zoomed through the intersection; another vehicle hit the back of, Angela's vehicle at an awkward angel, which caused, Angela's car to spin out of control before she could regain control another car hit hers pin balling her around. The second collision put, Angela's car back on track. She stomped down on the pedal and picked up speed. "Talk to me Troy!"

"He's four cars ahead of you," Troy said as he sweated profusely as if he was the one behind the wheel and not, Angela.

Angela grazed two more cars as she ran into the back of another one. "Sorry!" she said out loud, as she quickly weaved around the car and picked up speed. Sweat was now pouring down her face; whatever, Angela had been injected with was definitely doing its job because she could barely keep her eyes open.

"Okay make a right at the next light," Troy's voice echoed in, Angela's ear. Angela cut the wheel hard to the left as another car tapped her bumper from behind causing her car to spin out of control and flip upside down several times before finally coming to a brutal stop. As, Angela went in and out of consciousness, she could feel someone pulling her out of the vehicle. Two men dressed in all black quickly pulled, Angela out of the car, hand cuffed her, threw a black pillowcase over her head, then violently tossed her in the back of a van then pulled off.

SEVEN

WHO ARE YOU?

Matt Hardy weaved the big man's knife strike and landed a strong open-hand chop to the big man's throat. The big man took the blow well, lifted, Matt Hardy off his feet, and drove him down hard to the floor. While on the floor, Matt was able to grab the big man's arm and forced him to shove the knife down into his own shoulder.

"Arghh!" the big man howled in pain as he watched, Matt Hardy hop up off the floor. Matt landed a quick eight-punch combination to the big man's face then finished him off by snapping his neck. Matt Hardy took a second to catch his breath, but when he looked up, he saw a beautiful woman standing in front of him with a gun pointed at his head.

"Who are you?" Matt asked with his hands up in surrender.

"That's not important!" Ashley said quickly. "Just know that I know who you are agent Matt Hardy."

"It's not what it seems," Matt said. "I'm doing this so I can get close to, the Lion and finally bring him down once and for all."

"Bullshit!" Ashley snapped. "You ain't nothing but a traitor. Now get down on your knees!"

"Listen," Matt Hardy began. "We have about one minute before a bunch on guards bust up in here and kill the both of us."

Psst!

Ashley fired a shot inches away from Matt's head to let him know that she meant business. "Down on your knees the next one I won't miss."

Matt slowly got down on his knees. "We got about twenty more seconds."

"Shut up," Ashley barked as she grabbed the briefcase off the floor and examined it. "What's in this briefcase that's so important that you're willing to risk your life to get it back to, the Lion?"

Before, Matt could respond, the door was kicked open and six guards stormed the room holding assault rifles. "Drop your weapon and the briefcase now!"

Ashley hesitantly dropped her weapon along with the briefcase then looked over at, Matt who had a calm look on his face. Matt quickly pulled a knife from the small of his back and threw it in the direction of the leader of the pack. The knife landed in the throat of the front man of the pack. Matt Hardy dove on the floor and came up holding,

Ashley's gun. He quickly put down two of the gunmen with headshots. Ashley ran and rushed the gunman closest to her and tackled him down to the floor. One of the guards ran over towards, Ashley and aimed his gun at her head but before he could pull the trigger. His head exploded, splattering blood and brain matter all over the wall. The last gunman turned and tried to make a run for the exit but was quickly shot from behind several times.

Ashley muscled the gun away from the gunman, placed the barrel under his chin, and pulled the trigger. Her face was immediately showered with blood. Ashley stood to her feet, spun around, and saw, Matt standing there with a gun aimed at her head.

"Put that gun down," Matt said calmly as he watched Ashley do as she was told. He then reached down, removed a pair of handcuffs from off one the guard's belt, and tossed them to, Ashley. "Here cuff yourself to that wall unit!"

Ashley caught the handcuffs and did as she was told. "You're making a big mistake."

"It's not what you think," Matt Hardy said. "You'll understand later," he turned, grabbed, Ashley's cell phone, pressed a few buttons, tossed the phone down to the floor, then made his exit. Matt reached the hallway and disappeared in the staircase where he was met by two more guards. Matt Hardy shot the first guard in the face at close range. The second gunman knocked the gun out of, Matt's hand and threw a strong right hook. Matt ducked the punch, landed a powerful punch in the guard's gut, and then slammed the guard's head into the wall knocking him unconscious. Matt Hardy then continued on the down the stairs like nothing happened.

***

Ashley removed her back up .22 from her crotch and shot herself free, kicked off her heels, and quickly exited the room. Ashley entered the staircase and immediately spotted blood everywhere and two guards laid out on the floor. Ashley made it down one flight when the door busted open and a guard grabbed her in a bear hug from behind and lifted, Ashley off her feet. He tried to throw, Ashley down the stairs but she hung on to him taking both of them on a violent ride down an entire flight of stairs. When they finally landed at the bottom of the stairs, Ashley was fortunate enough to land on top she quickly removed a small four-inch blade from her bra and slit the guard's throat from ear to ear, causing blood to spray all over her face. Ashley quickly hopped to her feet and exited the staircase. Ashley reached the lobby and speed walked to the exit. Once outside she jogged towards the van. "Where's Angela?" she asked as soon as she stepped foot inside the van.

"She's gone. They took her," Troy said with a sad look on his face.

"Who took her?"

"The Lion."

EIGHT

WHERE AM I?

Angela woke up and found herself hanging by her wrist. Her wrist were bound together by a chain, someone had lifted her three feet off the floor and attached the chain to some type of hook. As, Angela hung freely from the hook, she looked down and saw dried up blood on her thighs. She also felt a burning and stinging sensation around her anus area. She had no idea what had been done to her while she was unconscious and honestly, she didn't want to know. Angela looked around for a way out or something that she could turn into a potential weapon but the dim lighting made it hard for her to see. After hanging for about thirty minutes, Angela heard a door open followed by the lights coming on. She squinted as she looked over in the direction of the door. The first person Angela recognized was, Roxy, followed by, Matt Hardy, along with several other soldiers. Seconds later, Angela spotted the man that she had been chasing step into the room. The Lion stepped in the room wearing an all-black expensive looking suit and a serious look on his face; he walked right up to, Angela and stared at her for a second.

"So," the Lion began. "You're the Teflon Queen that I've heard so much about," he looked her up and down. "What do you and your organization know about me?"

Angela stared at, the Lion and remained silent seeing him up close and person sent chills down her spine, she didn't know what it was about, the Lion but it was something about him that screamed trouble.

"What were you doing at that hotel?" the Lion asked.

"No comprenda," Angela replied sarcastically. The Lion reached up and roughly grabbed, Angela's cheeks and squeezed them together. "Whether you like it or not you're going to talk." the Lion turned to, Roxy. "Make her talk."

Roxy smiled. "My pleasure," she said as she lit up the fireplace, then removed a hunting knife and held it over the fire until the tip turned bright red. Angela looked down at the knife in, Roxy's hand, took a deep breath, and prepared herself for the pain that she knew was sure to follow.

Roxy walked up to, Angela and placed the tip of the hot blade on, Angela's stomach, immediately she could hear the sound of the flesh burning. Roxy smiled as she dragged the knife from, Angela's stomach down to her torso.

"Argh!" Angela howled in pain as she felt the hot knife carving her up. Matt Hardy looked on from the sideline with a disgusted look on his face. He didn't personally know, Angela but he had heard plenty of stories about the Teflon Queen. Matt Hardy pulled his cell phone from his pocket and sent off a quick text message then slipped his phone back down into his pocket.

After carving, Angela up, and still not being able to make her talk, Roxy had to move on to the next method of torture. Roxy removed a blowtorch from a dusty looking duffle bag; hit a button, and a bright orange and blue flame appeared.

The Lion walked up to, Angela. "What do you and your organization know about me?"

Angela cleared her throat and spat in, the Lion's face. The Lion wiped his face then turned and looked at Roxy. "Continue."

Roxy slowly walked towards, Angela with the blowtorch in her hand.

NINE

WE DON'T HAVE A CHOICE

Ashley and, Troy sat in their hotel room trying to figure out a way to locate, Angela's whereabouts but all of their resources lead to a dead end.

"You think she's still alive?" Troy asked. From the look on his face, one could tell that he had been up all night worrying.

"She's still alive. Angela is as tough as they come," Ashley said confidently. "We just have to find her before it is too late."

As, Ashley sat there in deep thought, she heard her phone vibrate; she looked down at the screen and saw a message from an unknown number. The message was simple, "Your friend is in big trouble right now!" Ashley read the message and knew exactly whom it was from. "Matt Hardy just texted me," Ashley handed the phone to, Troy. "Track the number so we can find the location to where they are."

"What if it's a trap?" Troy said. "What if he's trying to lure you into a trap?"

"Matt Hardy could have killed me the other night if he wanted to, but he didn't," Ashley pointed out. "Maybe he's trying to help?"

"Trying to help?" Troy echoed. "The man is a traitor he turned his back on his country and you think he's trying to help?"

"It may be a shot in the dark but it's the only shot we have right now," Ashley replied. Troy punched a few buttons on his keyboard then looked up from his screen. "The phone is a four hour ride from here." Troy wasn't too fond of heading to a location blind but if, Ashley trusted Matt Hardy, he was sure she had a good reason. Now with, Angela missing, it was his job to back her up and make sure she didn't get herself killed in the process of rescuing, Angela.

"What's the location?" Ashley asked as she packed her bag with all of the equipment that she was going to need.

"It looks like a raggedy warehouse but they must be holding her underground," Troy said. "You sure we can trust Matt?"

Ashley didn't reply instead she looked over at, Troy and winked.

TEN

WHERE IS SHE?

Ashley arrived at the location, and instead of it being a warehouse, the place looked an old run down mansion. Immediately, Ashley knew she was at the right location when she spotted three heavily armed guards standing out front. Dressed in all black, Ashley moved like a thief in the night as she moved closer and closer towards the entrance without being seen.

"Be careful they have cameras in front," Troy's

voice echoed through, Ashely's earpiece.

The three guards stood out front smoking cigarettes and telling your momma jokes when they saw a figure in all black appear out of nowhere.

Ashley dropped all three guards with headshots in rapid succession before they had a chance to reach for their weapons. Ashley then raised her weapon and shot the security camera. "Three tangos down. I'm moving in." Ashley said as she reached the side of the building and saw a pipe, without hesitation, Ashley grabbed onto the pipe and began climbing up the side of the building; she leaped from the pipe and grabbed a hold of the window seal. Hanging freely from the window seal, Ashley inched her way over towards the cracked window that resided in the middle of the building.

Troy looked on with a nervous and scared look on his face as he watched, Ashley hanging from the window seal. Ashley reached the slightly opened window and quickly pulled herself inside. "I'm in,"

Ashley said as she pulled her 9mm with a silencer attached from her holster and held it with a two handed grip. Ashley stepped out the room and spotted an armed guard with his back turn to her. Ashley quickly grabbed the guard from behind and placed the barrel to the back of his head. "Move and I'll blow your head off!" she growled into the guard's ear as she shoved him forward. Ashley made sure she kept her body positioned behind the guard so she could use him as a human shield if need be. Ashley spun around the corner and saw two guards sharing a laugh she quickly dropped both guards with headshots as three more guards came flying around the corner. The guard's opened fire without hesitation. Ashley returned fire as the guard she used as a shield body jerked and jumped with each bullet that entered his body. Ashley tossed the dead guard's body down to the floor as she picked up one of the guard's machine guns off the floor and took cover behind a wall. Seconds later several guards entered the room with murderous looks in their eyes and assault Ruffles in their hands.

"I'm going to need a little help here Troy," Ashley whispered.

"Coming right up," Troy replied as he shut down the lights in the entire building.

Once the lights went out, Ashley slid her night vision goggles down over her eyes and made her move. She used the darkness to her advantage as she walked through the room picking off soldiers left and right. Ashley could see a green silhouette from each guard's body from behind her night vision goggles making it easy to hit her targets. Ashley eased her way through the house when she was grabbed from behind and roughly slammed down to the floor. Ashley quickly hopped back up to her feet, ducked the guard's right hook, and came up with a sharp elbow that landed on the guard's temple. The blow staggered the guard but he somehow kept his footing. Ashley removed a knife from the small of her back and jammed the blade deep down into the guard's throat. Before that guard's body even hit the floor, Ashley looked up and saw another guard come flying around the corner with an A.K. 47 in his hand.

"Shit!" Ashley cursed as she took off down the hall in a sprint as a trail of bullets followed her every move decorating the wall just above her head. The guard held his finger down on the trigger as he aimed the A.K. in Ashley's path. Ashley sprinted at a low hunch having no other choice, Ashley was forced to dive through the window in the same motion she reached her arm out and grabbed a hold of the ledge with one hand. "Argh!" Ashley groaned as she hung on to the ledge for dear life with one hand. As, Ashley hung suspended in the air she quickly used her other hand and grabbed onto the ledge. When the guard came and looked out the window Ashley's hand shot up and grabbed the guard by his chest and tossed the guard out the window. Ashley looked on as she watched the guard fall to his death. Ashley used all her might to pull herself back up through the window; she quickly picked up one of the guard's weapons and continued on throughout the mansion.

ELEVEN

I DON'T THINK SO

The Lion looked on as, Roxy tortured, the Teflon Queen with a smile on his face. The Lion knew it would only be a matter of time before they broke her down and forced her to talk, he had heard plenty of violent stories about the so called Teflon Queen so seeing her in the flesh meant that the authorities must of been closer to him than he thought. Now he needed, Angela to talk so he could know just how much they knew about him and his operation.

Angela hung from her wrist dangling through the air. They had tortured her so much that her body couldn't take no more and shut down.

"She's passed out!" Roxy exclaimed with an aggravated look on her face, she badly wanted to kill, Angela and get it over with before they wind up regretting it later.

"When she wakes up finish the job," the Lion said in a stern tone. "We need to find out who she's working for and what she knows."

A guard peeked his head in the room. "Your chopper just landed on the roof boss," he whispered to, the Lion.

The Lion nodded his head. "I have to go take care of something," he looked up at Roxy. "I don't care what you have to do make her talk!" the Lion said as suddenly all the lights went out.

Matt Hardy quickly grabbed, the Lion. "Come on we have to get you out of here!" he said as he rushed, the Lion into the staircase. As Matt Hardy and, the Lion headed up the stairs towards the roof, Matt Hardy thought about taking, the Lion out and getting it over with. He knew he would be doing the world a big favor. Matt Hardy tried to talk himself out of taking, the Lion's life but the urge was just too tempting. Without warning, Matt Hardy grabbed, the Lion from behind and violently rammed his head into the wall. Matt Hardy followed up with a powerful left-right combination. The first punch landed flush, But, the Lion blocked the second blow and landed a quick three-punch combo of his own. The last blow landed on Matt Hardy's chin and stunned him. The Lion took advantage he went low and landed a good body shot. The Lion smiled as he watched, Matt Hardy double over in pain, not giving him a chance to recover, the Lion spun and landed a roundhouse kick to the side of, Matt Hardy's head that sent him crashing down the stairs. Just as, the Lion was about to finish, Matt Hardy off, the staircase door busted open and a gunman dressed in all black emerged holding a big machine gun.

"Shit!" the Lion cursed as he dove down a flight of stairs just as the gunman opened fire.

Ashley eased her way down the stairs, she kept one hand on her weapon and used her other hand to help, Matt Hardy up to his feet. Ashley reached down, pulled her back up 9mm from a holster, and handed it to, Matt along with a small flash light. Ashley eased down the stairs with caution she knew, the Lion was one of the most dangerous men in America. Ashley eased the door open and stepped out into the hallway when her feet were immediately swept from under her causing her to drop her weapon as she hit the floor hard. The Lion stepped down on, Ashley's neck, just as he was about to apply pressure the staircase door swung open and, Matt Hardy fired a shot into, the Lion's chest. The impact from the shot spun, the Lion around in the same motion. He landed a roundhouse kick that sent, Matt Hardy's gun flying from his hand. Ashley jumped up from off the floor and charged, the Lion she threw several blows all, which, the Lion blocked with ease and countered with a knee to Ashley's rib cage, the Lion then used, Ashley's momentum against her and tossed her head first into the nearest wall. Matt Hardy quickly grabbed, the Lion from behind and threw him in a chokehold. Immediately, the Lion backpedaled violently ramming, Matt Hardy's back into the wall forcing him to release his grip. The Lion turned and landed a quick four-punch combination to, Matt Hardy's face. Matt Hardy blocked two of the blow but the other two managed to slip through. Matt Hardy took the blows well and threw several of his own. Ashley looked up from the floor and saw, the Lion and, Matt Hardy going blow for blow in a loud noisy fight. Ashley quickly joined in. The Lion blocked and dodged blows coming from both, Matt

Hardy and, Ashley. While, the Lion and, Matt Hardy went at it Ashley grabbed, the Lion from behind and took him down to the floor they squirmed around on the floor until, Ashley was finally able to wrap her legs around, the Lion's neck in a scissors hold she immediately began to apply pressure. The Lion quickly grabbed, Ashley's legs and tried to pry them from around his neck as his face turned bright red. Ashley got ready to snap, the Lion's neck when out of nowhere, Roxy came busting through the staircase door with a machine gun in her hand.

"Shit!" Ashley cursed as she released her grip from, the Lion's neck and quickly hopped back up to her feet before she got a chance to make another move. Roxy squeezed down on the trigger. Ashley stood there like a deer stuck in the headlights when, Matt Hardy tackled her into the next room just as the loud thunderous sound of rapid gunfire filled the air.

Roxy helped, the Lion up to his feet quickly as the two disappeared into the staircase and made their way up to the roof where the chopper awaited them.

"Hold on!" the Lion said as he stopped and pulled out his cell phone and hit a button and a three-minute countdown began. "Come on we have to get out of here in three minutes this place is going to explode!

Ashley rolled over, looked at, Matt Hardy, and saw that he was bleeding. "Oh my god are you hit?"

"Yeah one must have went through," Matt knocked on his vest for extra emphasis.

"You have three minutes to find, Angela and get out of there before the entire building explodes!" Troy's voice barked into, Ashley's earpiece. Ashley turned and faced, Matt Hardy. "We have to three minutes to find Angela before the building explodes."

"Follow me I know exactly where she is!" Matt

Hardy said as he led the way. Matt escorted, Ashley to a room down in the basement. Ashley opened the door and spotted, Angela hanging by her by wrist. From all the scars and blood that covered, Angela's body, Ashley could only imagine the pain she had endured. Matt Hardy quickly pulled, Angela down from the chains.

"I knew you were coming," Angela said as she flashed a bloody smile. Matt Hardy tried to lift, Angela over his head but stopped half way when his bullet wound didn't agree with the attempt.

"I got her!" Ashley said as she tossed, Angela over her shoulder like a wounded troop in the army, and then quickly headed for the exit.

"Forty-five seconds!" Troy said with urgency. Matt Hardy sprinted towards the exit as fast as he could. Ashley did her best to keep up the only problem was the place was so big that the exit seemed miles away. Her chest heaved up and down as her legs worked in over time there was no way she was going to let, Angela go out like that. Ashley made it twenty feet from the exit when she heard a loud boom, followed by the ceiling collapsing. Residue from the ceiling landed on top of her head as well as Angela's body. Ashley just made it out the front door when a loud explosion sounded off loudly behind her. The force from the explosion hurled, Ashley and, Angela's body forty yards away. Ashley's body violently landed in the middle of the street an oncoming car had to stomp down on the brakes and swerve to the left to avoid running the woman that laid in the middle of the street over.

Meanwhile, Angela's body slammed violently into a tree then landed on the unforgiving concrete.

Ashley looked up and saw, Matt Hardy standing over her. He quickly helped her up to her feet and escorted Ashley over to the van that just pulled up. Troy hopped out the van and helped, Ashley inside. Troy looked up at Matt. "Where's, Angela?"

"I think she landed over there somewhere," Matt

said as he watched, Troy head over in that direction. Troy walked over towards the grass where he found, Angela laid unconscious looking like she had just been tossed out a window. He quickly picked up and brought her back over to the van. Once Troy made sure that, Angela was secure in the van, he quickly got behind the wheel and burnt rubber away from the scene.

TWELVE

THANK YOU

"You think she's going to be okay?" Troy asked with a scared look on his face as him and, Ashley sat around, Angela's bed.

"She's going to be fine she just needs to rest," Ashley replied with a concerned look on her face. It bothered, Ashley to see, Angela like this.

"I'm just happy that we got her back alive," Troy said. He knew how dangerous their job was, at any minute any one of them could have been killed so each day above ground is appreciated and not taken for granted. "How do we go about finding, the Lion now?"

Ashley shrugged. "Your guess is as good as mine."

"You think, Matt Hardy may know something?" Troy asked.

"It's possible," Ashley said. "I'm sure, the Lion wants him dead we can maybe use him for bait."

"I don't know if that'll be a good idea especially with, Angela out of commission," Troy pointed out. "I don't even think it's safe for him to be in the same hotel as us being as though he's got a bulls eye on his back."

"I'll call, Mary Wiggings and see what she has to say," Ashley picked up her phone and dialed, Mary's number.

Mary answered on the second ring, "Ashley, talk to me."

"We found, the Lion but he managed to get

away," Ashley explained. She still didn't fully know what was going on and figured she'd get some answers while she had, Mary on the phone. "Do you have any more info on, the Lion?"

"Why do you ask that?"

"Because he's well trained in the combat area and there's only a few places a man like him could get training like that from," Ashley pointed out. After fighting with, the Lion, she immediately knew that he wasn't your average terrorist; he actually had some real skills.

"Actually we just got a little more info on, the Lion. Comes to find out he used to be one of us," Mary said. "His real name is, William Woods but he's had plastic surgery done on his face that's why we didn't pick it up from the jump. The Lion used to be one of the best field agents ever until about five years ago when he went on a mission and just vanished that's why it's so urgent that we find agent, Matt Hardy we believe, the Lion may be recruiting,

Matt Hardy to follow in his footsteps and go against his country."

"Matt Hardy is in the same hotel as us, he's not a traitor he actually saved my life as well as, Angela's life." Ashley said honestly. "He said he was working undercover so he could learn, the Lion's system and take him out."

"Text me your location right now!" Mary said her tone changing from friendly to serious. "Agent Hardy is a very dangerous man and you can't believe a word he says keep an eye on him I'm sending a unit to bring him in."

"I'll keep an eye on him until the unit arrives," Ashley said. "I'll be with him so make sure your unit holds their fire."

"I can assure you that there will be no shots fired," Mary said in an even tone. "Keep, Matt Hardy on ice until the unit arrives."

"No problem," Ashley ended the call.

Mary hung up the phone and quickly dialed

another number. On the third ring, a male's voice answered. "Yeah."

"I have, Matt Hardy's whereabouts. I knew we couldn't trust him," Mary huffed. "You're going to have to get a new face because by the morning every agent in the country will have your sketch."

The Lion paused before he replied. "I'll take care of, Matt Hardy Ashley, and, the Teflon Queen," the Lion said in a calm tone.

"You better because if this blows up in my face it's not going to be pretty," Mary warned him.

"I said I'll take care of it," the Lion said then ended the call.

THIRTEEN

WHAT DID YOU TELL HER?

Matt Hardy sat in his room cleaning his gunshot wound with alcohol, then wrapped a fresh gauze over it. Last but not least, he popped a few pain pills and proceeded to clean his baby Uzi with the extended clip. After cleaning his weapons, Matt leaned his head back and decided to rest his eyes for a second. He had been up for the past seventy-two hours and his body badly needed the rest. Matt Hardy sat up in the chair resting with his Five-Seven handgun with in arms reach when he heard a light knock at the door. He immediately sat up, grabbed his gun off the table and made his way towards the door. "Who is it?" he yelled.

"Ashley," the voice on the other side of the door called back. Matt Hardy slid his gun back down in his holster, opened the door, and stepped to the side so, Ashley could enter.

"Hey we need to talk," Ashley said as she helped herself to a seat on the couch and crossed her legs.

"I'm all ears," Matt said as he sat back in his original seat.

"What's your story?" Ashley said. "And don't bullshit me I want the truth."

"Where do I begin?"

"From the beginning please," Ashley said with an attitude.

"When I first joined TSA I was assigned to find, the Lion and eliminate him," Matt Hardy began.

"Every time I would get his whereabouts he would always slip through the cracks somehow. It was as if someone was tipping him off so one day I got a tail on, the Lion's main hit woman Roxy. I followed her and I could of taken her out but I decided to befriend her hoping I could get in good with her and maybe she could lead me to, the Lion," Matt paused to take a sip of water. "At this time I still had never seen his face and no one in the department even knew what he looked like. After doing a few jobs with Roxy she trusted me then I was finally allowed to meet, the Lion."

"Did you kill any innocent people?" Ashley asked.

"Plenty," Matt Hardy answered truthfully. "I was taught to sacrifice a few people in order to save millions."

"Okay so what happened when you finally met, the Lion?" Ashley asked.

"I met, the Lion and to my surprise he was a

pretty nice guy, a serious guy, but overall a nice guy, that is until you cross him," Matt said. "He welcomed me in with open arms and gave me anything I asked for; money is no object to a man like him. But what I did notice was every time he took his phone calls he took them in private, but one time he took a call and walked into the other room but kept the door open and I was able to read his lips and I heard him ask whoever he was talking to do they know who I really am so he definitely has someone on the inside helping him out. We just don't know who yet."

"What do you know about Mary Wiggings?"

"Not much ever since I went rogue she tried calling me a few times but I never answered her because I knew there was a mole on the team and I wasn't sure who it was," Matt Hardy said honestly. "I don't know what it is about, Mary but it's something about her that I don't trust," Matt took another sip of his water. "But what about you what's your story?"

"Well I was sent here to eliminate you and, the Lion, but after our first encounter I knew you weren't who they were saying you were," Ashley admitted. "I knew you were still on the right team."

Matt leaned over and kissed Ashley on the lips. "When I saw you, you were so beautiful there was no way I could harm you," he said as he kissed her again but this time it was with more passion. Ashley immediately spread her legs and pulled, Matt down on top of her. Ashely quickly removed her holster along with her black slacks and tossed them onto the floor. Matt's eyes lit up when he looked down and saw all of that thickness waiting for him. Without warning, Matt reached down and ripped, Ashley's thong off like a barbarian. Ashley moaned loudly when she felt, Matt's tongue flickering on her clit. Matt took his time and licked and slurped all over, Ashley's peach loudly. Ashley released a moan from deep down within she hadn't been pleased by a man in such a long time that it felt unreal. Ashley wrapped her legs around, Matt's neck she wanted to keep him there forever and live in the moment. Matt raised from in between, Ashley's legs and roughly turned her over on her stomach and took her from behind. Matt slid in and out of, Ashley at a steady but firm pace pleasing her with each and every stroke. Ashley moaned loudly as she grabbed a fist full of the sheets, arched her back, and let, Matt Hardy have his way with her. After two back-to-back intense lovemaking sessions, Ashley laid down and fell asleep in Matt's arms. The two enjoyed a nice nap until they were awaking by the sound of, Ashley's cell phone ringing. Ashley rolled over when she heard her cell phone ringing. "Hello?"

"Ashley its Mary do you still have Matt Hardy in your sites?" Mary asked.

"Yeah why?"

"Good keep him in your sites the unit will be

there to pick him up in five minutes."

"Okay," Ashley ended the call then turned and look at Matt. "That was, Mary she said a unit will be here to pick you up in five minutes."

Matt Hardy sat straight up with an intense look on his face. "You told her where I was?"

"Yes just tell them what you told me and you'll be fine," Ashley said. "Just tell them the truth."

Matt Hardy jumped up and quickly began to get dressed. "Are you crazy?" He yelled. "I just told you, the Lion has someone working for him on the inside! Until I find out who the mole is I'm staying off the grid!" he said as he grabbed his twin baby Uzis and slipped them down into his shoulder holsters that rested below his armpits. Ashley quickly threw her clothes on, grabbed her weapon, and, followed, Matt out the door.

"Matt why don't you wait and see if they can help you?" Ashley suggested.

"I betrayed the Lion he's not going to rest until

I'm six feet under the ground!" Matt Hardy barked as he stepped out of the hotel. "Ain't no telling who he's got working for him!"

Ashley followed, Matt into the underground garage she felt that maybe, Matt was over reacting a little bit but it was better to be safe than sorry. "Where are you going to go?"

Matt Hardy shrugged. "I don't know but far from here and I suggest you do the same!"

Ashley went to say something else when a bullet ripped through her shoulder and spun her down to the ground. Matt looked up and saw three men heading in their direction in a low crunch he quickly removed his twin Uzis from his holsters and returned fire. The gunmen quickly split up and took cover behind parked cars. "You alright?"

"Yeah it went in and out," Ashley said as if getting shot in the shoulder wasn't a big deal. She pulled her gun from the holster and held it tightly as the sound of engines revving filled the garage. Matt looked up and saw six more gunmen on motorcycles enter the garage. "Come on we have to go!" Matt yelled as he smashed his elbow into the driver's window of a parked car and let himself inside, and then popped the locks so, Ashley could get in. Ashley ran around to the other side of the car and shot one of the gunmen in the face, she slid in the passenger seat of the vehicle not even waiting to see the gunman's body hit the floor.

Matt hotwired the vehicle, threw the gear in drive, and stomped down on the gas pedal just as the back window shattered. "Hang on!" Matt said as he swerved through the underground garage at a high speed. Ashley hung out the window and fired six shots in rapid succession. Matt peeked up at rear view mirror and watched three of the gunmen fall violently off their bikes as bullets from, Ashley's gun invaded their personal space. Matt cut the wheel hard to left forcing, Ashley's to jerk to the right. Up ahead one of the gunmen on a motorcycle called himself playing chicken with, Matt.

"Put your seat belt on!" Matt Hardy said as he stomped down on the gas pedal causing the vehicle to pick up on speed. When the gunman saw the vehicle pick up speed, he did the same the engine on his bike sounding like a speedboat. The car and motorcycle collided like two Rams.

Matt watched with a blank expression in his face as the gunman bounced off the front windshield shattering it in the process. Matt Hardy cut the wheel hard to the right as a silenced bullet ripped through the windshield and hit him in the face splattering his blood all over the window.

"Matt? Matt?" Ashley called out frantically as, Matt's head laid slumped over the steering wheel. She reached out to grab the steering wheel but before she could get control of the wheel the vehicle crashed into a wall, the air bag popped out and smashed, Ashley in the face. Ashley looked up and could immediately feel blood trickling down her face she used her hand and reached around the floor until she found her gun.

Several gunman slowly surrounded the crashed vehicle and opened fire sending over a hundred bullets into the body of the vehicle.

FOURTEEN

KILL EVERYONE

Mary Wiggings stepped out of a black suburban followed by, the Lion. She smiled when she heard through her walkie-talkie that, Ashley and, Matt Hardy had just been gunned down. "Now that those two are out the way I want, the Teflon Queen dead!"

"My men will handle her," the Lion said confidently. "Besides, she's only about twenty percent right now. My team did a real number on her back at the warehouse,"

"You sure they can handle her?" Mary asked with a look of concern on her face.

"I'm positive," the Lion said as he and, Mary got back into their vehicle and removed themselves from the murder scene.

Fifteen gunman entered the hotel with murderous looks on their faces. The leader of the pack walked right up to the front counter and shoved a big ass gun in face of the desk clerk. Once he had the info he was looking for him and his fourteen violent friends made their way up to, Angela's room.

***

Troy jumped out of his seat when he heard the deadly sound of machine gunfire from the window. Immediately his mind went to, Ashley he hoped and prayed that she was alright and not on the receiving end of those gunshots. Troy grabbed his 9mm from off the coffee table and quickly pushed, Angela's hospital like bed out into the hallway.

"What's going on?" Angela asked waking up from her sleep when she felt her bed moving. Troy ignored, Angela and knocked on the door across from them. Seconds later a tiny Chinese woman opened the door.

"Yes?" the Chinese woman asked as her eyes went from, Troy to the woman lying on the bed with several bandages covering her body.

Troy moved his hand from behind his back and aimed his gun in the Chinese lady's face. "Ma'am step aside we need to use your room for a second." He said forcing his way inside the room. Troy grabbed the woman by the collar of her shirt and placed his gun to her ribs, then whispered, "Listen to me carefully if you make a sound I will kill you sit down and keep your mouth shut and we'll be out of here before you know it do you understand?"

The Chinese woman nodded her head yes then

helped herself to a seat on the couch.

"Now are you going to tell me what the hell is going on and where's, Ashley?" Angela winced in pain as she sat up with a concerned look on her face.

"Long story. I'll explain later," Troy said in a low whisper as he walked over to the door and looked through the peephole. Angela pulled herself off the bed and stood to her feet. She knew she was too weak to do any major work but there was no way she was just going to lay there while they were in trouble. "Toss me a gun!" Angela whispered. Troy reached down in the small of his back and tossed, Angela a .380. Angela caught the gun, cocked a round into the chamber, then took cover behind a wall; she looked over at the Chinese woman and placed a finger up to her lips reminding her to keep quiet.

Troy watched from the peephole as several men kicked in the door across the hall and stormed inside their old room.

The leader of the pack entered the room and found it strange that the room was empty. He looked around and saw a few bloody bandages in the garbage which could only mean that Angela couldn't have been far. "They're around here somewhere!" he barked as he exited the room and stood out in the hallway. The leader of the pack stood there for a second before he walked over to the room across the hall and knocked on the door.

Troy watched through the peephole as the head gunman knocked on the door. Troy slowly placed the barrel of his gun at the door around the same place where the gunman's head stood on the other side of the door. Troy's gun followed the gunman's head like a magnet. Just as, Troy was about to pull the trigger, he noticed the gunman step away from the door and head back into the room. Troy was about to breathe a sigh of relief when he noticed their former room go up in flames through the peephole. Troy slowly walked over to, Angela. "We're going to have to get out of here. They just set the room on fire."

"Shit!" Angela whispered. She looked down at her feet and remembered that she didn't have any shoes on. As, Troy and, Angela stood there trying to come up with their next move, the Chinese woman jumped up off the couch and sprinted towards the door. Before either, one of them could stop her, the Chinese woman was already out the door. Troy went to go chase after the woman when two gunmen busted inside the room. Troy turned his gun on the first gunman, but he was quickly tackled down to the floor. Angela thought about taking the shot but it wouldn't be a clean one. Before she had time, two other gunmen came busting through the door but were quickly stopped dead in their tracks by headshots from, Angela's pistol. Angela limped over towards where, Troy and the gunman were tussling on the floor. Angela knew that, Troy wasn't much of a fighter so she knew he needed her help. Angela raised her leg to stomp the gunman's head into the floor but just as her leg was on the way down another gunman came busting through the door, running at full speed he got low and hit, Angela hard in her gut with his body, his momentum sending the both of them stumbling backwards and crashing through the glass door that led out onto the balcony. Angela hit the floor and immediately dug her nails into the gunman's eyes and tried to dig them out.

"Arggh!" The gunman growled as, Angela flipped him over onto his back and rained down several blows to his exposed face. The gunman easily bucked his hips and tossed, Angela off of him. The gunman stood to his feet and landed a four-punch combination to, Angela's face and head. Angela landed a jab of her own that caused the gunman's head to snap back she followed up with a wild right hook, but the gunman ducked it easily and delivered a crushing uppercut to Angela's rib cage. The impact from the blow caused, Angela to drop down to her knees. The gunman then grabbed the back of, Angela's head and tried to knee her in the face, but, Angela was able to block the knee and land a blow of her own to the gunman's groin. Angela stumbled back to her feet with a frustrated look on her face. She knew that if she was functioning at a hundred percent she would of been gotten rid of the gunman but do to all of her injuries she found herself in a fight for her life. The gunman grabbed, Angela by the throat and tried to choke the life out of her. Angela struggled trying to remove the death grip that the gunman had around her throat. Angela felt herself losing consciousness when she delivered a knee in between the gunman's legs then bent down, lifted him up over her shoulder, and flipped him over the balcony.

Angela stumbled back inside the room and saw the gunman on top of, Troy trying to strangle the life out of him. Angela walked over, picked up her gun, and shot the gunman in his face.

"Ew!" Troy groaned as he pushed the gunman's dead body off top of him and wiped the dead man's blood from his face. "Thank you." Troy picked his gun up from off the floor and peeped his head out the door. "Coast looks clear we have to move fast!"

Angela stepped out into the hallway with a firm grip on her gun and a bad limp. Angela led the way down the hallway while all the other guests ran out of their rooms with the fear of burning to death. The thick black smoke made it hard for, Angela to see. Angela made her way down the hallway when she saw what looked like a gunman. She quickly grabbed, Troy's hand, blended in with the rest of the crowd, and entered the staircase. Angela coughed loudly as she looked over at Troy. "We have to find, Ashley!"

FIFTEEN

STAY ALIVE

Several gunman surrounded the wrecked vehicle with their weapons aimed at it. A brave gunman walked over to the vehicle and snatched the driver's door open. "She's gone!" he announced with a surprised look on his face. The head gunman looked up and saw three of his fellow soldiers that stood next to him grunt, grab a body part, and then drop down to the ground.

"Get down!" he yelled at him and the remaining

gunmen split up and took cover behind three different parked cars.

Ashley moved at a low crunch with a firm grip on her pistol. She counted three gunmen in total. Ashley laid down flat on her side and fired off two shots. One of her bullets exploded in one of the gunman's ankles sending him crashing down to the floor in pain. Once the gunman hit the floor, he was in, Ashley's line of fire. It wasn't long before a bullet hit him right between the eyes snapping his head back, silencing him forever. Ashley crept around behind another parked car where she spotted another gunman with his back turned to her. With the quietness of a cat, Ashley crept on the gunman from behind and snapped his neck with ease she then laid his body down quietly on the cement hoping not to draw the attention of the last remaining gunman. Ashley tiptoed quietly around another car when she looked up she saw the reflection of the last remaining gunman creeping up on her from behind through the paint of a car. Ashley's eyes opened wide in fear when she realized that the gunman was right behind her. Ashley closed her and prepared herself for the pain that she was sure to come next.

POW!

Ashley opened her eyes and quickly spun around only to see, Angela standing over the gunman's body holding a smoking gun in her hand.

"Happy to see me?" Angela said with a smile. Ashley quickly ran over to, Angela and gave her a tight hug.

"We don't have much time we have to get out of here," Troy said breaking up the woman's embrace. Troy broke into an all-black charger, hotwired it, and peeled out of the parking garage like a bat out of hell, never looking back.

***

Ashley looked out the rear window, breathed a sigh of relief she knew how close she and her entire team had just come to death, and was thankful to still be above ground. Ashley looked over to, Angela. "You okay?"

"I'm still alive," Angela replied as she took two BC powders straight to help ease some of her pain. "What happened to, Matt Hardy?"

Ashley's eyes went down to the floor. "He didn't make it."

Angela draped her arm around, Ashley's neck. "I'm sorry."

"He saved my life," Ashley said as a tear escaped her eye.

"How did, the Lion and his people find us?" Angela asked as she rested her eyes and leaned her head back.

"Mary Wiggings," Ashley said with fire dancing in her eyes. Because of Mary, an agent had been murdered in cold blood as well as a lot of innocent people.

"Don't worry, we'll find her," Troy said

speaking for the first time as he continued to focus on the road.

The trio checked into a low budget motel in the middle of nowhere. Once they had settled in, Troy volunteered to get rid of the stolen car that was parked out front. Once, Troy was gone, Angela turned to, Ashley and rubbed her back. "I'm sorry about, Matt,"

"It's not your fault," Ashley sniffed as the tears continued to stream down her face.

"You really liked him huh?" Angela asked as she noticed the pain visibly in, Ashley's face. Ashley nodded her head. Angela knew exactly what, Ashley was going through. In their line of business, it was hard to find someone who you could call a friend, let alone one of the opposite sex. Angela felt bad for, Ashley especially since she was much younger than she was. "You ever thought about getting out of this life and trying to live a normal life?"

Ashley shook her head no. "I probably wouldn't even know how to be normal if I tried," she said in a defeated tone as if her living a normal life wasn't an option. "With all the evil that's going on out here I don't think I'd be able to just turn my back and go on living a normal life I already know too much."

"Ashley you are still young and have your entire life ahead of you," Angela pointed out.

"I just feel empty inside," Ashley said honestly. Here she was in her early twenties and still hadn't been in a real relationship. "I have no family no kids all I have is you; you're the only family I have."

The more Ashley talked, the more it made Angela think about her former lover, James, and all the things she had been missing out on in life as well. "We're going to be okay," she rubbed Ashley's back as they both heard Troy enter the room. "How'd it go?"

"I say we have about three to four days until someone finds that car," Troy answered. When he looked up, he noticed, Ashley wiping her eyes and Angela sitting with a sad look on her face. "What's wrong?" He helped himself to a seat on the couch.

"Just girl talk," Angela said not wanting to volunteer, Ashley's personal business. She looked up at the television and the look on her face instantly changed. "Turn that up!"

Ashley grabbed the remote off the couch and turned up the volume. A picture of Ashley, Troy, and, Angela was posted on the screen with the words 'armed and dangerous' under it.

"Armed and dangerous," the reporter began. "These three are said to be responsible for the massacre of over thirty dead innocent people found in the hotel and parking garage behind me," the reporter continued with a serious look on her face. "Also I'm being told a bombing just took place at a corporate building downtown about forty five minutes ago and these three are the main suspects. I'll bring you more as the story continues to develop."

Ashley cut the TV off and threw the remote against the wall out of frustration. "Mary is trying to make it seem like we're the terrorist to cover her ass."

"The best way to confuse the general public is through the media," Angela shook her head.

"Well there goes our resources," Troy announced. With the entire world thinking that they were terrorists there was no way that would be able to call for help.

"Captain Spiller would never turn his back on us," Ashley said confidently.

"There's only one way to find out," Angela tossed, Ashley the burner phone.

SIXTEEN

DON'T MAKE ME LOOK STUPID

Captain Spiller sat in a meeting with a sour look on his face. He couldn't believe what he was hearing, he sat in the meeting with a neutral look on his face, but on the inside, he was furious.

"Captain Spiller are you okay?" Mary Wiggings asked as she stood up before the entire room.

"Yes I'm fine I'm just having a hard believing what I'm hearing," Captain Spiller admitted.

"Well I'm sure this is a hard pill for all of us to

swallow," Mary said with a phony smile. "But I was there and saw with my own eyes."

"And what exactly did you see again?"

"Like I said before I spoke to agent Ashley over the phone," Mary began for the fifth time. "She told me she had agent, Matt Hardy in her possession. I told her I would be there shortly with a team to apprehend him when my team and me got there we found, Matt Hardy, Ashley, and her entire team trying to make an escape. My team identified themselves then we were fired upon," Mary paused to take a sip of water. "We were able to take down agent, Matt Hardy but, Ashley and the rest of her team managed to escape not before killing over thirty of my best men."

"I have a hard time believing that," Captain Spiller told her. "My team took this mission as a favor to help you out," he pointed out.

"Captain Spiller, when you met, Angela, the so called Teflon Queen," Mary said making air quotes with her fingers. "Wasn't she serving a life sentence for murdering over sixty people, law enforcement included?"

"That's correct," Captain Spiller answered, knowing exactly where, Mary was going with this.

"Then why is what I'm telling you so hard to believe?" she asked. "Your team is armed and dangerous and I'm issuing a T.O.S (Terminate on Site) to be put out immediately!"

Captain Spiller nodded his head. "Are we about done here?" he asked as he felt his back up burner phone that only a few people had the number to vibrating in his pocket.

"Yes we are," Mary replied with a smirk.

"Bitch," Captain Spiller mumbled under his breath as he exited the meeting and answered his phone. "Yeah"

"Hey captain, it's me, Ashley,"

"This better be damn good!" Captain Spiller growled into the phone. "What the hell is going on?"

"Mary is working with, the Lion and tried to set us all up to be killed but we managed to escape," Ashley explained.

"I figured that," Captain Spiller peeked over his shoulder to make sure no one was within ear distance of him. "Mary just issued a T.O.S out on you three so be careful and try to fly under the radar."

"I need to know everything you have on, the Lion so we can take him down before he hurts anymore innocent people," Ashley pressed.

"I don't know much, but what I do know is that he and a few of his soldiers just landed in New York this morning, and then just suddenly disappeared out the clear blue sky," Captain Spiller explained. "I don't know what he and his team is up to, but I'm guessing it's something big you and, Angela have to stop him before he can destroy anything else."

"We're on our way to New York now!" Ashley said then ended the call.

SEVENTEEN

NEW YORK

The Lion sat in the back of a yellow cab along with his number one hit woman, Roxy. He wore a wool skullcap on his head and a fake beard and mustache to try and hide his true identity. "You ready?"

Roxy nodded her head. The look on her face was a no nonsense one, she lived for action and couldn't wait to blow some shit up.

"Are your men already in position?" the Lion

asked.

Roxy nodded her head. "Yes, they're just waiting on my call."

The Lion smiled as him and, Roxy stepped out of the cab and disappeared down the steps towards the subway. In, Roxy's hand, she held a cell phone she quickly sent off a text message before she lost service underground.

The Lion's second in command, a soldier who went by the name, Scar. He got the name because of the long scar that went from his ear down to his chin. Scar looked down at his phone and saw the message from, Roxy he then turned to the six soldiers that had orders to do exactly as he told them. Scar stood on the platform, took a long drag from his cigarette, then flicked it to the ground as he saw the train approaching. Scar and his six soldiers boarded the train then patiently waited for it to take off. Once the train was in motion, Scar made his move. Without warning, he pulled an A.K. 47 from the guitar case he held and opened fire on several innocent people that happened to be at the wrong place at the wrong time. The six soldiers then violently grabbed the remaining people on the train and roughly forced them all to the last cart on the train. While the soldiers did that, Scar made his way to the conductor's booth. He raised his A.K. and sent ten rounds through the door. Scar then snatched the door open and watched as the conductor's lifeless body fell down to the floor. Scar pulled a walkie-talkie from the small of his back and spoke into it. "We're in!"

***

Once Roxy got the word from Scar, she and, the Lion made their move. Roxy made her way down to the platform where she saw three more of, the Lion's soldiers. Roxy pulled a 9mm from her waistband and shot the first seven people she saw in cold blood.

"Everybody down on the floor now!" Roxy

yelled, and then fired four loud thunderous shots up into the air causing everyone on the platform to get low and drop down to the floor out of fear. Another one of, the Lion's soldiers began to set up a camera and tripod. The Lion removed his trench coat and revealed the Kevlar vest that was strapped to his chest along with the two chrome handguns that rested under his arms in the holster. Roxy and two other soldiers rounded up all the hostages and made them all lay face down on the cold cement. The Lion then sent, Roxy on her way so she could get ready for the second phase of their plan.

The Lion stood in front of the camera and when the man standing behind the camera gave him a hand signal, the Lion began. "Greeting world," he began with a serious stone look on his face. "I'm going to make this short and sweet! I want twenty billion delivered to one of my off shore accounts you have twenty-four hours to deliver," he paused for a second. "I have around seventy hostages.

Every hour I will kill one hostage and please don't try and come down here because the place is rigged with explosives and I will blow this place up and anything within a twenty-block radius! Don't fuck with me!" the Lion barked. "Also I've took over one of the trains that's also holding over seventy passengers. That train is also packed with explosives and trust me when I tell you my men won't hesitate to blow that train out the sky," the Lion threatened. "America you have twenty-four fucking hours to get me my money!" the Lion then turned and snatched a female hostage off the floor by her hair and pulled her up to her feet, he pulled a gun from his holster, placed it to the side of the woman's head, and pulled the trigger. "Twenty-four hours!" the Lion barked with specs of blood covering his face. The cameraman stopped the video and sent it to every news station in several different countries as well as uploaded it to YouTube. Another one of, the Lion's soldiers hopped up from off the train tracks with a cheesy smile on his face. "All the bombs are in place we're all set."

"Good now if anyone of these hostages tries to make a move you kill em!" the Lion ordered.

EIGHTEEN

YOU HAVE TO STOP THEM

Angela sat in the back of the stolen van with a serious look on her face. After watching the news and seeing, the Lion's video, she knew she couldn't allow him to blow up the subway station. Angela was dressed in all black and prepared to do whatever she had to in order to put a stop to, the Lion's evil plan. She was only sixty-five to seventy percent healthy but for now that would have to do.

"You sure you're going to be able to handle

this?" Troy asked with a concerned look on her face. He knew the kind of condition, Angela was in and was a little worried about her.

Angela flashed Troy a smile. "I'll be fine. You just make sure you keep me updated on, Ashley."

"Between the two of you I'm going to have gray hair before my time," Troy huffed as he pulled the van over on a deserted block. Angela hopped out the back of the van and walked over to the sewer, stuck a long pipe that resembled a crowbar down onto the sewer lid, and quickly removed it not trying to draw any attention.

Troy walked over and hugged Angela tightly. "I won't be able to communicate with you through the air piece as usual because if we use the air pieces then headquarters will be able to track your location and every move, but here," Troy handed her a black mask that would cover her entire face. "Put this mask on and to hide your identity just in case of any cameras and on top of this mask is a camera so I'll be able to see your every move. I'll communicate with you on my computer and you'll be able to read my messages from off of your watch," he handed her a watch. "The watch won't make a sound but it will slightly buzz on your wrist to notify you that you have received a message."

Angela placed the watch on her wrist and slid the mask down over her face. She winked at, Troy, and then slowly climbed down the manhole. Troy placed the lid back over the manhole and prayed that, Angela would be okay.

***

Ashley walked up the last flight of stairs in the abandoned warehouse and pushed the door open to the roof. As soon as the door opened, two men immediately shoved guns in her face. Ashley slowly threw her hands up in surrender. "What the hell is going on here?"

"Lower your weapons please," Captain Spiller ordered with a serious look on his face. From first glance, Ashley could tell that he hadn't had any sleep in a couple of days. "Ashley get over here!" he barked. "I don't know what the hell is going on or how you and Angela are going to fix this!"

"I have to stop that train," Ashley said. She too was dressed in all black and ready to stop, the Lion and ruin his plan by any means necessary.

"Where's Angela?" Captain Spiller asked.

"She's down at the subway," Ashley answered.

"I don't even want to hear any more. Y'all just do what y'all have to do," Captain Spiller shook his head, he knew if one thing went wrong that he would lose his job as well as his freedom. He watched, Ashley board the chopper. From that point on, all he could do was pray that nothing went wrong.

***

Angela dropped down into the sewer water with a loud splash. The smell of urine, mixed with shit, and throw up immediately attacked, Angela's nostrils and almost caused her to gag. Angela pulled her Five-Seven pistol from her holster and held it with a tight grip as she pulled the night vision goggles down over her eyes so she could see in the dark. Angela made her way through the dark tunnel as rats took turns running across her feet. Angela reached a dead end and climbed up a metal ladder that led to the second level. She reached the second level and could immediately hear chatter followed by loud laughter. Angela held her pistol with a two handed grip as she felt a light vibration on her wrist from her watch. She raised her wrist and saw a message from Troy. "Three heavily armed tangos up ahead. Be careful."

Angela pulled a silencer from one of her pockets and screwed it onto the barrel of her gun, then slowly eased her way around the corner. Angela crept up on one of the gunmen from behind with ease she used the darkness to her advantage.

One of the gunmen stood digging in his nose

when out of nowhere, a gloved hand clamped down over his mouth and a gun was placed to the side of his head. A light splash of water grabbed the two other gunmen attention. They looked up and the last thing they saw was the muzzle flash. The gunmen dropped quickly making a loud splash. Angela held the gunman in a chokehold and whispered in his ear. "Where is, the Lion?"

"He's up on the platform," the gunman answered. "Please don't kill me."

"What were y'all doing down here?" Angela asked as she noticed something plastered to the wall with a green light blinking on it. "What is that over there?"

"A bomb!" the gunman growled.

"How many of those are down here?"

"Twenty!"

"Shit!" Angela cursed. "How do I defuse these bombs?"

"Fuck you!" the gunman growled as he

delivered an elbow to Angela's ribs then tried to make a run for it, but two bullets exploded in his back before he could even make it ten feet away. Angela took a deep breath. The blow to the ribs had really hurt her especially since she wasn't a hundred percent to begin with. Angela felt a buzz on her wrist then looked down at her watch and saw another message from, Troy. "You're making too much noise two tangos are on 'their way around the corner headed your way!"

Angela got down on one knee, steadied her gun, and waited. Seconds later, two gunmen came running around the corner and were immediately put down with headshots. She then typed Troy a quick message. "I have to defuse these bombs and I need you to walk me through it."

Angela walked over to the bomb and studied it carefully. She had no clue what she was looking at. Seconds later, she got another buzz on her wrist from, Troy giving her instructions on how to disable the bomb. Angela flicked the blade open on her

108

knife and carefully did as, Troy had instructed. The light on the bomb went from green to red notifying Angela that she had successfully disabled the bomb. "One down and nineteen to go," she whispered to herself.

NINETEEN

FIGURE IT OUT

Ashley sat on the helicopter with a nervous look on her face. She knew that a lot was riding on if she succeeded or failed and in her mind failing wasn't an option. "We're coming up on the train now!" the pilot announced. He too wore a nervous look on his face. Ashley took a deep breath as she took a second to mentally prepare herself for what was going to come next. After saying a quick prayer, Ashley connected the cord to a strap on her waist, and then turned towards the pilot. "Keep it steady!" She yelled as she snatched open the door and looked down at the moving train down below. Ashley slowly began to lower herself down from the helicopter. Ashley lowered herself half way down when she looked up and saw that the train was headed into a tunnel, which meant she had to move fast. "Shit!" Ashley cursed as she lowered herself down even quicker. As she was lowering herself down onto the train, Ashley looked up and saw a news helicopter flying in the air filming the entire thing. Ashley continued to lower herself down when her cord stopped. "What the hell?" Ashley said to herself with a confused look on her face as she fumbled around with the cord. The cord jammed leaving, Ashley suspended twenty feet above the train. Ashley looked up and saw the first cart of the train had already entered the tunnel. "Shit!" Ashley cursed as she removed a knife from the small of her back and cut herself free from the cord. Ashley dropped twenty feet down onto the top of the train just as it went completely underground. If she had missed her jump by one second, she would have been dead. Ashley hung onto the top of the train for dear life as the coach moved around sixty miles an hour. Ashley laid face down on top of the moving train for a few seconds so she could get comfortable with the train's movements. On a silent count of three, Ashley slowly slid down in between the train carts, and peeked through the window and saw that the cart window that she was looking through was empty. Ashley slid the door open and boarded the train with a two handed grip on her Five-Seven pistol with a silencer attached to the barrel. She slowly made her way from cart to cart until she reached the cart before the last one. Ashley moved at a low crunch until she made her way to the door, she slowly peeked her head up and spotted several gunmen holding the hostages at gunpoint. Ashley quickly snatched open the door leading to the next cart catching everyone off guard. By the time the gunmen looked up and knew what was going on it was too late Ashley had already rewarded them all with headshots. "Everyone remain calm and shortly I'll get you all to safety!" Ashley announced to the hostages. While, Ashley was talking a brave strong, muscular passenger called himself trying to save the day, he quickly grabbed, Ashley from behind in a bear hug then violently slammed her face first down to the floor. Ashley wiggled out of the big man's grip and landed a combination of blows to the man's head and throat area she then finished him off with a roundhouse to the temple that put the big man on his back. Ashley went to reach for her gun when the big man swept her legs from under her. The big man then roughly snatched, Ashley up to her feet and rushed her back into the door. The force was so hard that, Ashley's head went straight through the small window. Having no other choice, Ashley bit down on the big man's finger forcing him to release his grip on her, she then landed a series of blows to the man's head, then tackled him violently down to the floor where she finished him off by grabbing the man's ankle and giving it a deadly twist. The loud sound of the man's bone snapping followed by a loud scream filled the train. "Anyone else what some?" Ashley asked looking around at the hostages. "I'm here to save y'all now let me do my job!" She barked. Ashley picked her gun up from off the floor. "I need all of you to stay put and don't move until this train comes to a complete stop!" she ordered as he exited the cart and headed towards the front of the train.

***

Scar sat in the conductor's booth when he heard a loud scream. "What the hell?" he said to himself as he pulled out his walkie-talkie and tried to radio his soldiers. After a few times of not getting a response, Scar decided to take matters into his own hands. Scar grabbed his A.K. 47, exited the conductor's booth, and headed towards the last cart where the hostages were held. Scar sensed that something was wrong so he kept a strong two-handed grip on his weapon as he moved from cart to cart with caution. As, Scar reached the last cart, he came to a stop when he noticed blood smeared on the window. Scar leaned his head to the right to get a better look inside the cart. Immediately, he saw the look of fear on the hostages faces. Scar took a step forward when he felt the barrel of a gun being pressed into the back of his skull.

"Drop the weapon...now!" Ashley growled with venom dripping from her tone.

"You're making a big mistake," Scar said as he dropped his weapon, placing his hands in the air. "I'm willing to die today. Are you?"

"Shut the fuck up!"

"Two choices sweetie," Scar said as he slowly spun around. Ashley's gun was now placed at his forehead. "One, you can turn and get the hell out of here, or two we can both die today. The choice is yours."

"I think I'm going to have to take choice number two," was, Ashley's response. Without warning, Scar swept his hand across the gun, moving his head in the opposite direction at the same instant, the gun discharged into the ceiling. As, Scar struggled to rip the gun out of Ashley's hands, the gun fired over and over again. Ashley managed to slip her leg behind, Scar's leg and took him down to the floor with ease the fall caused both of them to lose possession of the gun.

Scar quickly bounced back to his feet, removed a sharp hunting knife from the small of his back, and charged, Ashley like an attack dog. Without thinking twice, Ashley flicked open the blade on her knife and charged at Scar. Scar tried to stab, Ashley short range, but, Ashley used her good footwork to get out of striking distance barely making it out of stabbing range. She grabbed, Scar's wrist and sliced him across the face forcing him to drop his knife. Ashley went to stab Scar in the chest but he landed a rabbit punch to, Ashley's temple the blow stunned her, caused her legs to wobble, but the next blow put, Ashley flat on her back. Ashley shook the blow off and climbed back up to her feet just in time to see Scar crossing from one cart to the next.

Scar exit the next cart and climbed up the small ladder that led to the outside of the train. He quickly crawled to the roof of the train and laid flat on his stomach while the train moved at a fast speed underground. Having no other choice, he had to find an escape plan now that, the Lion's plan had been compromised. Once the train came from underground, Scar stood to his feet, he looked up and saw a helicopter hovering over above him. Scar looked down and saw nothing but water beneath him. There was no doubt in his mind he was going to jump for it and take his chances.

"Put your hands up or else we will open fire!" the announcement came from the helicopter. Scar ignored the announcement and got ready to jump off the moving train, but just as he was about to take that leap, Ashley tackled him down on the roof of the train. Down on his back, Scar fought for his life, he reached up and wrapped his hands around, Ashley's throat and tried to strangle her to death.

"You have ten seconds to surrender or else we will open fire!" the second announcement came from the helicopter.

Ashley dug her fingers into, Scar's eyes, forcing him to release his grip from around her neck. Ashley quickly made it back to her feet, spun, Scar around, and threw him in a choke hold when the sound of loud machine gunfire ripped through the air. Several bullets ripped through, Scar's chest and stomach area riddling him with bullets. Having no other choice, Ashley tossed, Scar's lifeless body off the train, and then dived head first off the top of the train just as the helicopter opened fire again. It seemed as if she was floating through the air in slow motion before finally landing in the water making a loud splash.

TWENTY

KILL HIM

"Take three steps to your right and you can't miss it," Angela read, Troy's message from off her wrist. She followed his instructions and found the last bomb resting behind a huge pipe. Angela carefully disabled the bomb then headed for the platform. Angela made her way towards where she saw lights and knew she was getting closer, her adrenaline pumped as her palms got sweaty, and her stomach began to do little flips.

Angela looked down at her wrist when she felt another vibration. "Be careful, the Lion and his men are heavily armed...good luck!"

Angela quickly replied. "I'll be fine any word on, Ashley?"

"Not yet!"

***

The Lion stood on the platform with an intense look on his face he had been trying to get in contact with Scar for the last thirty minutes with no such luck. The Lion knew that something bad must have happened to, Scar because he was too smart to betray or turn his back on him. The longer, the Lion had to wait to get in contact with, Scar the angrier he was becoming. The Lion turned to the gunman that he hired to watch his back twenty-four hours and seven days a week a soldier who went by the name, Razor. "Any word from, Scar yet?"

"Not yet I'll try him again," Razor said as he pulled out his phone. Razor punched a few keys on his phone, lifted the phone up to his ear then lowered it and shook his head. "Nothing!"

The Lion calmly looked down at his watch. "One hour is up! "he growled as he stormed over and roughly snatched one of the hostages up to his feet. "Cut the camera on!" he yelled. The cameraman quickly did as he was told, not wanting to get on, the Lion's bad side. Once the camera was rolling, the Lion put on a hell of a show.

"It's been an hour and I still don't have the money in my account! You Americans must think I'm playing. I guess I'm going to have to show you better than I can tell you! The Lion pressed the gun to the back of the hostage's head and pulled the trigger causing all the rest of the hostages to scream out in fear.

"You think I'm playing!" the Lion yelled. "You want to fuck with me!" He ran over, snatched up another hostage, and blew her brains all over the camera for extra emphasis. "Thirty minutes to get that money into my account or else I kill another hostage!"

After, the Lion's speech, the cameraman cut off the camera, cleaned off the lens, then sent the video to all the news stations as well as uploaded the video to YouTube and social media.

The Lion turned to, Razor. "Get ready to blow this place if these fuckers don't transfer that money into my account within the next hour. We're going to blow this place!"

"The authorities' think they have several more hours to come up with the money because of how many hostages we have," Razor pointed out.

"I don't trust these people and I'm not going to sit around and give them time to come up with a plan to put a bullet in my head!" the Lion lightly scolded him. "Now go check on the bomb and make sure we all good to go," the Lion ordered.

Razor quickly went off to do as he was told. He hopped down onto the train tracks and made his way down the tunnel. As, Razor made his way down the tunnel he stepped in something wet where a guard was supposed to be stationed. Razor pulled out his pen light, shone the light down to the ground, and saw what looked like blood. He slowly bent down on one knee, touched the substance, and felt that it was still warm which meant that the blood had been spilled not too long ago. Razor pulled his 9mm from his holster in a snapping motion. He had been trained by the best of the best and was well capable of killing and even better at surviving. Razor had been bored lately because of the lack of action, but now he had a good feeling he was about to be knee deep in the action. Razor slowly made his way over towards the first bomb and saw that it had been disabled. Razor then checked the next two bombs and saw that those too had also been disabled. Razor quickly pulled out his walkie-talkie and radioed in to, the Lion. "We've got company. Someone disabled all the bombs!"

Razor yelled into his walkie-talkie as a bullet exploded in his back. "Arghh!" Razor grunted as he dropped down into the disgusting sewer water and returned fire.

Blocka! Blocka! Blocka! Blocka!

Razor quickly made it back to his feet and scanned the area from left to right to see where the gunshot came from. Razor heard movement coming from his left; he quickly turned to the left and opened fire. Razor dropped the clip out the base of his gun and jammed a fresh clip inside in point two seconds. He took cautious steps towards where he heard the noise coming from when out of nowhere, he was tackled down the floor and a knife was jammed into his shoulder. Razor quickly kicked the mask man off of him. Razor made it half way back on his feet when the mask man delivered a series of fist and elbow strikes to his face. Razor tried to block the blows but several of them managed to slip through his guards. Having no other choice, Razor went low and scooped the mask man's legs from up under him and dumped him head first into the sewer water.

Angela's head bounced off the floor under water but she couldn't let that stop her she had to continue to fight. Angela wiggled out of, Razor's grip and landed an upper cut to his rib cage Angela made it back to her feet and took a fighter's stance. Razor charged at Angela like a wild bull swinging wildly and with bad intentions, each blow had knock out written all over it. Angela blocked and weaved every last blow that, Razor threw and fired back a few stiff blows of her own. Both of their hands were moving so fast it looked as if the two were fighting in a Kung-Fu movie. Angela landed blow after blow to, Razor's exposed face then landed a standing sidekick that landed square on his chin. The kicked caused, Razor to stumble but he somehow managed to keep his footing. Angela landed a jab that snapped, Razor's head back then slipped behind him and threw him in a chokehold. Razor quickly back peddled, ramming, Angela's back into the concrete wall but still Angela didn't release her grip from around his neck. Razor repeatedly rammed, Angela's back into the wall trying to force her to release her grip from around his neck. Angela tightened her grip around, Razor's neck, hopped up on his back, wrapped her legs around his waist, then took him down into the sewer water and applied even more pressure to the chokehold. Razor's arms and legs wailed back and forth as he desperately tried to get some air but it was no use Angela's death grip was just too tight. Angela continued to apply pressure until Razor finally stopped moving. Angela crawled back to her feet, removed her back up gun from her thigh holster, and headed straight towards the platform.

***

The Lion stood on the platform with a stone look on his face and a gun in his hand. He heard

Razor's message and sent three more of his soldier down into the tunnel to help with the problem, but that was over ten minutes ago and he hadn't heard anything since but gunshots and loud pain filled screams. "Come on it's time to go!" the Lion yelled out to his last two soldiers that stood guarding his side. He reached over, snatched the A.K. 47 from the hands of one of his soldiers, and opened fire killing each and every last hostage. The Lion handed the assault rifle back to his soldier when, out of nowhere, the soldier standing next to him head exploded like a melon causing warm thick blood to splash all over, the Lion's face. He looked up and saw a masked gunman hop up onto the platform with a gun in his or her hand. Angela dropped the two remaining soldiers with head shots then turned her gun on, the Lion and pulled the trigger. The Lion weaved his head in the nick of time causing the bullet to miss his head and instead land into his shoulder. The impact from the shot caused him to spin around and stumble down to the floor. Angela stepped over several of the hostages dead bodies as the business end of her gun led her around the corner but there was no sign of, the Lion. Angela stood perfectly still for a second and used her ears to see if she could locate her target. Angela looked down at the ground and saw little dots of blood, which meant that, the Lion was wounded how badly was the question, Angela cautiously followed the blood trail. She moved cautiously across the platform when, the Lion appeared out of nowhere and hit her low, tackling her down onto the train tracks from off the platform. Angela's landing was hard, rough, awkward, and unforgiven. The Lion landed on top of, Angela and began raining blows down on her exposed face. Angela took the punches well as she reached up and jammed her finger through the hole in, the Lion's shoulder.

"Arghhhh!"the Lion howled in pain as he reached down and snatched the mask off the gunman's face, his eyes lit up and his face showed a shocked expression when he saw that the mask man was no other than the Teflon Queen. The Lion slapped, Angela's hand away as she bucked her midsection tossing him off of her. The Lion charged, Angela throwing a series of blow and kicks from all angles. Angela blocked most of the blows with her arms and elbows but, the Lion's blows were coming faster than her arms could block. The Lion landed a spinning back kick that landed in the center of Angela's chest the impact from the kick sent her crashing into the wall. Angela placed her back foot on the wall and lunged forwards landing a powerful punch to the bridge of, the Lion's nose. The Lion countered with a jab that snapped, Angela's head, he then grabbed her by the shoulders and jammed his knee into her already wounded rib cage. Angela landed a vicious head butt that shattered, the Lion's nose. The Lion pulled a throwing knife from the small of his back and tossed it at, Angela. The knife was coming straight for, Angela's face and out of instincts; she raised her hand to block the knife. "Arghhh!" Angela shrieked in pain as the knife lodged in the middle of her palm. "Shit!" Angela cursed as she watched blood spill from her hand. On a silent count of three, she snatched the blade from out the palm of her hand and let out a loud grunt. Angela spun around and saw, the Lion sprinting down the dark tunnel. Without thinking twice, Angela quickly took off after him.

***

The Lion sprinted down the dark tunnel at a steady pace. His body was well trained and used to running miles at a time so the long sprint didn't bother him one bit. What did bother him was the fact that the Teflon Queen had single handedly ruined his master plan before the funds were transferred into his account for that she would have to pay but right now, the Lion's main focus was escaping with his freedom. He looked behind him and didn't see, Angela but he knew that she wasn't far behind. The Lion ran until he reached the next platform. He quickly hopped up on the platform and shot the two cops that stood guard the sound of the loud gunshots sent the rest of the commuters in a frenzy making it easier for, the Lion to blend in with the crowd.

Angela hopped up on the platform and looked around but saw, the Lion nowhere in sight. She made sure she held her gun behind her leg as she moved through the commuters not to draw any attention to herself. As, Angela made her way through the station, her eyes scanned from left to right. Angela felt a vibration on her wrist and looked down at the message. "Go up the stairs and make a right...hurry!" Angela jogged up the steps and cut to the right in front of her were two signs "Uptown and Downtown"

Angela looked down at her wrist and the word

"Uptown," was staring at her. Angela made her way down to the uptown platform and all she saw was a sea of different faces. She moved throughout the crowd with cautious as her eyes continued to scan from left to right. Angela typed a quick message to, Troy. "Where is he?"

Angela squeezed through the crowd when a train pulled up to the platform. Hundreds of passengers exited the train while hundreds more boarded. Angela continued to make her way through the crowd when she received a message from, Troy. She looked down at her wrist and the message read. "He's on that train!" Angela quickly ran through the crowd of people and slid on the crowded train just as the doors were closing. Angela squeezed through the crowded train. She passed panhandlers and train performers who put on an entertaining show for tips. Angela bumped past an old Chinese lady who was selling batteries. She moved from one cart to the next with a firm grip on her weapon. Her hand badly burned and stung but,

Angela did her best to ignore the pain and remain focus on the mission at hand. She continued to move through the crowd then came to a complete stop when she spotted, the Lion standing in the very next cart.

The Lion looked over to his right and spotted the Teflon Queen standing in the next cart watching him with a stone cold look in her eyes. The train slowly came to a stop and when the doors opened, the Lion darted off the train smack dead into the middle of the crowd. When the train doors opened, Angela ran off the train, and pushed her way through the crowd of people and chased after, her target. Angela stopped short, looked around from left to right, and didn't see, the Lion nowhere in sight. Angela continued to make her way through the crowd but there were just too many people in the subway making it damn near impossible to spot, the Lion.

The Lion walked past a small shop, snatched a hat off the rack, slipped it on his head, and continued on about his business as if he was a regular law abiding citizen. He stood on the crowded platform and when the next train arrived, he gladly stepped on.

TWENTY-1

MAKE IT GO AWAY

Mary Wiggings sat in her luxury home enjoying a glass of white wine while watching CNN. Mary watched as the reporter explained in detail about the terrorist attack gone wrong. Deep down inside she knew that, Angela had something to do with the deactivation of the bombs. Mary hadn't heard from, the Lion yet and wasn't sure if he had escaped or been apprehended but either way there wasn't anything that could of led the authorities back to her. Now, Mary had to worry about, Angela coming after her. She had to come up with a plan that would eliminate, the Teflon Queen once and for all before this thing blew up in her face. Mary got up and walked towards the refrigerator to grab some more wine when a gloved hand clamped down over her mouth and the barrel of a gun was pressed into the back of her skull. "I knew you'd be coming," Mary said in a calm tone as she spun around and looked the gunman in the eyes. The Lion stood there with a gun pointed at her head.

"You told me you would take care of, the Teflon Queen!" the Lion growled as he turned and slapped, Mary down to the floor. "I've paid you a lot of money for your services and in return I've gotten nothing!" He kicked her in the ribs.

"Lion please I'll take care of it, I just need a little bit of time," Mary pleaded with blood running from her mouth. She knew what a man like, the

Lion was capable of and needed to do whatever she could to get off his bad side.

"I've gave you chance after chance," the Lion said in a calm tone. "Now I'm afraid your time is up."

"All I need is one more chance," Mary begged. "One week and I'll make all this go away!"

"You're lucky I like you," the Lion slipped his gun back into his shoulder holster. "You have a week to get rid of, the Teflon Queen and to have those funds transferred into my account or be prepared to suffer the consequences."

"Thank you," Mary said with a look of relief on her face. She knew that, the Lion was well trained and as violent as they came. She stood to her feet. "Come here let me look at you," Mary said, as she examined, the Lion's broken nose. She also spotted what looked like blood by his shoulder. "Oh my god you've been shot!"

"Just a flesh wound," the Lion downplayed the

severity of his injury. The Lion looked in, Mary's eyes as he used his hand to open up her silk bathrobe. Mary's perky breast stood at attention as, the Lion leaned down and tasted her nipples. Mary let out a soft moan as she felt, the Lion's fingers slowly climb in between her legs and began to massage her love button. Next thing you know the two were on the floor butt naked. The Lion laid, Mary on her back and pinned her legs back towards her head as he roughly rammed himself in and out of her wetness. Mary screamed out in ecstasy with each stroke that, the Lion delivered. When, the Lion was done handling his business he cleaned himself off and made his exit leaving, Mary there laying on the floor panting heavily from the mind blowing experience. Twenty minutes later, Mary picked herself up off the floor, and made her way over to her cell phone. She had a few calls to make.

TWENTY-2

WHAT'S NEXT?

Angela parked the stolen car down in the woods then continued on her journey by foot. She was dressed in all black, a hood covered her head and the strings were drawn tight making it damn near impossible to see her face. Angela moved swiftly but couldn't deny the fact that her body was in tremendous pain from her battle with, the Lion. Angela was still mad at herself for letting, the Lion get away. She was just glad that she was able to stop the bombing from taking place and save the city. Angela took a cab to her destination then swiftly walked a couple of blocks away to the run down motel that was now their headquarters. Angela entered the motel room with her gun drawn. With everything that had been going on you could never be too careful.

"It's just me," Troy with his hands raised. "Glad you made it back alive." Hegot up and hugged Angela tightly but not too tight assuming she had some injuries. "Good work."

"Thank you," Angela flashed a smile. It felt good to be back around someone she really trusted. "Any word from Ashley?"

"Yeah she's in the tub soaking," Troy replied. "Go have a word with her while I try and figure out how we can track down, the Lion. Angela walked over to the bathroom door and knocked gently. "Come in," the voice from behind the door called out. Angela stepped in the bathroom and saw,

Ashley sitting in a tub full of ice water up to her neck.

"How you feeling?"

Ashley flashed a weak smile. "Not too good but I'm still alive."

"You did good work earlier today. I'm proud of you," Angela complimented. She could tell that something was on, Ashley's mind.

"You were great too. I heard all about what you did on TV," Ashley said the expression on her face was the one of sadness.

"Talk to me Ashley. I can tell that something is wrong," Angela closed the lid on the toilet seat and sat down.

Ashley let out a long drawn out sigh. "For years I've been doing my best to try and serve my country and now just like that," she snapped her fingers. "I go from hero to fugitive."

"Don't worry we will clear our name before this is all said and done," Angela assured her. "Have you thought about what we talked about?"

"What living a normal life?" Ashley chuckled. "Yeah right. I don't even know what normal is," she admitted.

"I think you should give it a shot. You never know you may like it."

"That's not my focus right now right now. My only focus is killing, the Lion and getting rid of him once and for all," Ashley stated plainly. The two women turned when they heard a light knock on the door.

"Hey I think I found out how to get to, the Lion," Troy's voice echoed from the other side of the door. Ashley stepped out of the tub and covered her nakedness in a long towel as her and, Angela stepped out the bathroom together.

"What you got for us?" Angela asked as she helped herself to a seat next to, Troy. Angela looked at the computer screen and saw a handsome Caucasian male who looked to be British staring back at her.

"Tom Savage. He's, the Lion's accountant and adviser," Troy announced. "If anyone knows where to find, the Lion it's him."

"And where do we find this, Tom Savage?" Ashley asked.

"He just checked into the Hoxton Hotel in London," Troy replied. "He checks out in two days."

"With the amount of money that, the Lion was requesting, he must have something big that he's planning," Angela said out loud. "And he's definitely going to need his accountants help dealing with a large sum of money like that."

"Whatever he's planning you have to stop him and make sure that his plan never comes to life," Troy told her. "It looks like it's going to be up to us three to save the world from whatever this maniac has got planned."

"That's going to be a little difficult to do with

the three of us being wanted and the authorities having orders to shoot to kill," Ashley pointed out.

"That just means we have to move under the radar," Angela said as she began to pack for the trip.

TWENTY-3

YOU CAN'T DO THIS

Captain Spiller sat on his couch watching CNN with an angry look on his face. He knew he was in hot water but sometimes in life, you had to take chances and that's exactly what he did by communicating with Angela and, Ashley when he knew he wasn't supposed to. Captain Spiller was happy that, Angela and, Ashley were able to stop the bombings, but, the Lion was still out on the loose which meant at any moment he could strike again. Captain Spiller poured himself a strong drink and guzzled it down in one gulp as his face crumbled up from the burning sensation in his throat and chest. He poured himself another drink when his front door was kicked open and several men came storming in with guns aimed at his head.

Captain Spiller raised his hands in surrender. "What the hell is going on?" He looked around then paused when he saw, Mary Wiggings walk through the front door.

"Nice to see you again Captain Spiller," Mary said with a smirk. "Let's cut to the chase. Where's Angela and, Ashley hiding out at?"

Captain Spiller sipped his drink coolly. "How would I know?"

"Cut the shit!" Mary snapped. "You authorized for a helicopter to be on the roof the other day the same helicopter that lowered Ashley down onto that train,"

"I have no idea what you're talking about,"

Captain Spiller sipped again with a straight face. A strong faced officer placed, Captain Spiller's hands behind his back and cuffed him.

"Captain, we can either do this the easy way or the hard way the choice is yours," Mary looked him in the eyes.

"Just try not to mess up my good shirt," was Captain Spiller's response. One of the muscular agents rolled up the sleeves on his shirt and unloaded several hard punches to, Captain Spiller's exposed face.

Mary watched this go on for a few minutes before she stopped it. "Enough!" she yelled. "He's not going to talk. Take him to jail and let him rot," she ordered as she watched her agents roughly escort Captain Spiller out of his own home. With, Captain Spiller out the way, this would help make it easier to track down and kill, Angela and, Ashley. Mary knew that without, Captain Spiller's resources the duo wouldn't make it but so far. But what Mary was really hoping that the authorities caught Angela and Ashley before they got a chance to screw anything else up. Mary smiled as she watched Captain Spiller get carried away in the back of an unmarked vehicle. Now all she had to do was locate Angela and Ashley and eliminate them.

TWENTY-4

LONDON

Angela sat outside enjoying a nice meal at a five-star restaurant. To the average person, she looked like just a regular lady enjoying a nice meal on a nice day. Angela was seated two rows across from her target, Tom Savage. Tom Savage sat having lunch with a young blonde hair woman with bright red fingernails that he had just met the night before.

"So are you enjoying your stay in, London?"

Tom asked as he sipped his drink.

"I am but I think I'd enjoy you much more," the blonde flirted openly. "Are you always such a gentleman?"

"I try to be," Tom replied with a smile. Under the table, he felt the blonde rubbing her foot up his thigh.

"Tonight is my last night in town and I want to end my visit with a bang," she said in a seductive tone.

Tom wiped his mouth with his napkin. "I see," he quickly raised his hand and called for the waiter so he could get the check. "Don't let the clean look fool you. I can turn into a beast," Tom raised a brow. "You sure you want to bring the beast out of me?"

"Only one way to find out," The blonde replied as the two of them exited the restaurant and headed for his hotel room.

Tom and the blonde stepped on the elevator and

immediately the blonde pressed his back up against the wall and kissed him roughly, as her hand fondled the package in between his legs. "I'm going to tear you apart," she growled in his ear as the elevator dinged and the doors slid open. Tom Savage quickly stepped off the elevator and walked down the carpeted hallway until he reached his room. Tom removed his card key and let himself inside the room. "I hope you ready to back up all that talk because I'm about to...." His words got caught in his throat when he turned and found himself looking down the barrel of a gun.

Ashley pointed her gun at Tom's face, and then snatched the blonde wig off her head. "Have a seat!" she ordered as she shoved, Tom over towards the bed.

"What's this all about?" Tom asked in an arrogant tone. Ashley walked over to door and opened it as, Angela stepped in dressed in all black.

"Tom, I'm going to ask you simple questions

and I want some simple answers," Angela said as she handcuffed his hands behind his back. "Where is, the Lion?"

Tom chuckled, "I have no idea," he said with a smirk. The smirk was quickly removed from his face when, Angela filled his mouth with blood.

"Let's try this again, where is, the Lion?" Angela asked once more. Her tone was calm and relaxed.

"Un cuff me right this instant!" Tom demanded. He was rewarded with a swift kick to the face. Tom was then tackled roughly down to the floor and held there by Ashley. Angela stood over him and placed a towel over his face then proceeded to pour water over it. She repeated the process over and over until she felt that he'd had enough. Angela removed the wet towel from Tom's face and he immediately tried to suck up as much air as possible.

"Last time I'm going to ask you!" Angela growled. "Where's, the Lion?"

Tom laughed. "You have no idea what you're

about to get yourself into do you?" He looked Angela in the eyes. "Trust me," he paused. "You don't want to know where, the Lion is or what he's got planned. He will kill you and anyone else they send after him."

"Does it look like I'm joking around?" Angela challenged as she placed the towel back over Tom's face.

"Alright, alright, alright!" he yelled. "I'll tell you!" Angela roughly snatched him up to his feet and shoved him back on the bed.

"You better start talking!" Angela placed the barrel of her gun to, Tom's head she was running out of patience.

"The Lion is in Russia!" Tom confessed. "He's planning something real big!"

"What?"

"He's got an army of soldiers that's been trained by a former C.I.A. agent that's gone rogue and switched sides," Tom explained. "All of these soldiers are willing to do whatever he says. They're even willing to die for the cause if need be! They have all the same training that you all have and he's recruiting hundreds of soldiers by the day!" Tom explained. "He needed that money to be transferred into his account so he could fund the missions he would be sending them on."

"But isn't he a billionaire?" Ashley asked. "Why not use his own money?"

"The rich never use their own money," Tom looked at Ashley as if everyone should have knew that.

"So what's the Lion got planned in Russia?" Angela asked.

"Nothing that's just where all of his soldier's train at his facility. I know he's there now but I don't know how long he'll be there," Tom said.

"So let me get this straight," Ashley cut in. "So he's got an army of well-trained soldiers with no plan that doesn't make any sense to me."

Tom chuckled. "Do I have to explain everything to you two idiots, he's taking over all the smaller countries one by one until he's big enough to try and go to war with America he's been planning this for years. Now he's got Russia on his side it won't be long before he gets other countries to back him up once his army is big enough, so if y'all plan on stopping him y'all better move fast even now it may be too late."

"How many other countries has he met with?" Angela asked curiously.

Tom shook his head and gave Angela a disgusted look. "India, China, you name it and they're ready to back him! The Lion is like a god to everyone he goes to all those third world countries and give them water he's built schools he gives life to the people that has been looked over and counted out and in return they'll do anything for him his army is growing by the second," Tom explained. "Long story short of you don't stop, the Lion soon he's going to take over the world."

"So what's going on in Russia right now?" Ashley asked.

"A big meeting of all the most powerful men in world. The Lion is planning on winning them all over tonight at one of his mansions," Tom told them. "Oh and ladies I hope you have a small army on your side because you're going to need it."

TWENTY-5

RUSSIA

The Lion sat behind his oak wood desk in office with a bottle of vodka and a glass within arm's reach. Sitting across from him was, Mary Wiggings she was dressed in a nice expensive looking black dress, her face looked flawless, and red lipstick covered her full lips. "So any word on, the Teflon Queen?"

"Not as of yet but I'm sure we should be seeing her tonight," Mary smiled. She knew that, Angela had her way of getting to the bottom of things and crashing parties. "Like I told you we should be prepared for anything tonight we can't let her and her team ruin it for us."

The Lion nodded and poured himself a drink he took a slow sip. "I've got traps set up all around the building and my best men inside and outside of the building on high alert so I don't see anything or anyone being a problem tonight,"

"We should just be on point tonight just in case," Mary threw it out there.

The Lion flashed a smile as he stood to his feet he was dressed in a black tuxedo; anyone with a trained eye could see a gun under each one of his armpits. "Tonight is going to be a good night I can feel it," he downed his drink in one gulp only to refill his glass. "Shall we?"

The Lion and, Mary Wiggings stepped out of his office and walked down the long carpeted hallway in silence. The Lion turned the corner, walked down a few steps, and stepped into a room full of powerful men who patiently awaited his arrival.

"I thank you all for coming tonight is a special night," the Lion began with a smile. "Tonight we will form an alliance that will assure us so much power, enough power to run the world. With all the man power, resources, and all of our connections we will be u stoppable," the Lion stood before the crowd with a pleased look on his face. "I will be the face of this organization but we would all be equal partners therefore if anything was to happen to me the next man would easily step up to the plate. My face has been all over the TV and news so all of the heat will come down on me while the rest of you live your lives as normal. As long as we all work together, there will be no stopping us. We have people working for the FBI, CIA, as well as other government agencies. As long as we're all on the same page, there won't be no stopping us!" the Lion smiled as he sipped his drink he went to continue when he looked over to his left and saw, Roxy calling him over. "Excuse me," the Lion said with a smile as he walked over to the side with, Roxy.

"Looks like we have some company," Roxy pulled out a device that showed, Ashley snapping one of the guards at the front gate's neck she then hopped over the iron gate onto the property.

"Take care of her and make sure you bring, the Teflon Queen to me alive," the Lion ordered as he walked off.

"Will do!" Roxy said as she headed down stairs to find the trespasser.

***

Ashley hopped over the iron gate and landed down in the snow. She held a two-handed grip on her machine gun as she headed straight for the front door. Ashley made it close to the front entrance when the door came busting open; four gunmen came running out brandishing firearms. All four men were quickly copped down by bullets from, Ashley's machine gun. Ashley stepped over the dead bodies and entered the mansion. She looked up and saw what looked to be about twenty armed soldiers running down the stairs. Ashley opened fire hitting several of the soldiers as she dove behind a wall as several bullets lodged into the wall. On a silent count of three, Ashley got up and sprinted across the room as big holes decorated the wall in her path, Ashley did a front flip and rolled behind another wall. She waited for the gunfire to slow down before she sprang from behind the wall and put down several of the gunmen with headshots before ducking back down behind the wall. Ashley pulled a smoke grenade from her utility belt and tossed it over her shoulder. The grenade exploded filling the room with a thick coat of smoke. Ashley moved with the quickness of a cat as she moved through the room taking out gunmen one by one. She ran behind one of the gunmen and jammed a knife down into the side of his neck then gave it a deadly twist. Ashley moved swiftly throughout the room and put down four more gunmen before one of the gunmen grabbed her from behind and slammed her down on the floor. Ashley managed to muscle her way out of the man's grip and land a sharp hook to his temple she then quickly followed up with a four-punch combination her blows had no real effect on the gunman he took the blows well and landed four punches of his own. The gunman grabbed Ashley and violently threw her into the wall. Ashley bounced off the wall and landed a flying elbow to the gunman's face she then scooped his legs from up under him and dumped him on his head. The gunman lifted his legs and flipped, Ashley over his head. The gunman grabbed her then released her when he felt a stinging sensation he looked down and saw that he had been cut five times. Ashley stood with a bloody knife in her hand. The gunman swung a powerful right hook aimed at

Ashley's head. Ashley ducked the punch and jammed her knife in the middle of the gunman's chest. She looked him in his eyes as he took his last breath. Ashley pulled her 9mm from her holster and attached a silencer to the barrel as she continued on throughout the mansion.

***

Angela cautiously crept up on the side of the mansion she could hear the sound of several different guns being fired which meant that Ashley was doing her part. Angela tossed a rope that had a hook connected to the end of it up towards the second's story, she quickly pulled herself up the side of the building, grabbed on to the balcony, and pulled herself up. Once inside the mansion Angela pulled her Five-Seven pistol with the silencer attached to the barrel from her holster and moved cautiously throughout the mansion like a cat burglar. Angela tip toed down the hall and put a bullet in the back of one of the guard's head. She quickly grabbed the dead guard by the ankles and pulled him into one of the many rooms and out of plain sight. Angela stepped out the room and spotted two more guards in the middle of the hall. Before they knew what was going on they were put down by a series of silenced bullets. Angela stepped over the dead bodies and continued on throughout the mansion. Angela turned the corner and a bullet exploded into her vest causing her to stumble backwards.

"I've been waiting for you!" Roxy yelled, as she inched her way down the hall; in her hand, she held the same exact gun as, Angela. Roxy eased her way down the hall and placed her back up against the wall. On a silent count of three she sprung from behind the wall with her gun aimed ready to fire but, Angela was nowhere in sight. "Come out come out where ever you are!" Roxy sang as walked down the long hallway with extreme caution her eyes darted from left to right for any signs of movement. Angela sprang from behind a statue and dived through the door to one of the many rooms as, Roxy fired fifteen consecutive shots in her direction. Roxy removed the clip and placed a fresh one in her gun as she entered the room she had just saw Angela dive into. The room appeared to be empty but Roxy knew better. Roxy eased her way inside the room with seven soldiers behind her. "You're out-gunned and outnumbered!" she called out. "Surrender!"

Angela slowly stood up from behind the desk with her hands raised in surrender.

"Drop your weapon now!" Roxy ordered. Having no other choice Angela did as she was told and tossed her gun down to the floor. "Your back up weapon also!"

Angela removed the .380 from the small of her back and tossed it down to the floor. Roxy flashed a sickening smile. "Why would you come here knowing you were going to die?"

"I was hoping to take a few of you with me," Angela said with a smirk.

"I see," Roxy said with a smirk of her own. She too tossed her gun down to the floor. "Everyone stand down!" she ordered as she removed her shirt as well as her bulletproof vest. She stood before Angela in black fatigue pants, black combat boots, and a black sports bra. "Let's see if you're as good as they say you are," Roxy challenged as she got in a fighting stance. All of the soldiers in the room backed up and gave the two women room to get busy. Roxy inched towards, Angela and threw a jab that, Angela weaved easily and landed an upper cut followed by a hook to the ribs. Roxy took the blows well as she grabbed the back of, Angela's head and delivered a flying knee to her face. Angela blocked the second knee, lifted Roxy up over her head, and slammed her down onto the wooden desk.

BANG!

Angela tried to throw, Roxy in a chokehold but,

Roxy managed to somehow wiggle out of Angela's grip. Roxy smiled as she got on her tippy toes and began to bounce back and forth. She faked a jab and threw a straight left hand that landed in the center of, Angela's face, Roxy moved with blinding speed as she threw a quick combination of punches. Angela blocked many of the punches, but, Roxy's hand speed was proving to be too much for her. Roxy set, Angela up with a kick to the stomach then tried to finish her off with a roundhouse to the head. Angela ducked the kick, hit, Roxy while she was in the air, and then rushed her out of the room and rammed her back up against the wall. The two quickly hopped back up to their feet and continued to fight wildly all the way down the hall.

TWENTY-6

WHAT A PLEASANT SURPRISE

The Lion stood in front of a house full of guests when he heard a loud bang coming from upstairs. The Lion and all of his guest looked up and saw, Angela and, Roxy come spilling out into the hall way on the upper level of the mansion in an intense fight. "What a pleasant surprise," the Lion said with a smile as him and his guest looked up and watched the rather entertaining fight.

***

Angela grabbed, Roxy and belly to belly slammed her hard down to the floor. She rained down a series of fist and elbows down to, Roxy's face. Roxy flipped Angela off of her and rammed her foot into the pit of her stomach to give herself some breathing room. Roxy made it back to her feet, grabbed two handfuls of Angela's hair, and flung her violently into the wall. Roxy held Angela by the hair with one hand and landed several short blows to her face. Angela landed two blows to, Roxy's rib cage forcing her to release the grip on her hair. Roxy breathed heavily the long fight was beginning to take a toll on her but the thought of stopping never crossed her mind. Angela grabbed Roxy and tried to stomp down on her kneecap and break it but, Roxy managed to move her leg out the way just in time as she hip tossed, Angela down to the floor. Roxy grabbed, Angela's arm and put it in an arm bar. Angela tried to remove her arm but, Roxy locked her legs around, Angela's shoulder and began to apply pressure.

"Argggh!" Angela screamed as she felt the bone in her arm about to snap. Angela used her free hand, removed a small knife with a four-inch blade from one of her pocket, and jammed the blade in, Roxy's side causing her to release her arm in the process. Angela quickly stood to her feet, ran towards, Roxy, and hit her hard lifting her off her feet the two women hit the rail hard, and then flipped over it. Angela and, Roxy fell down to the lower level of the mansion and landed hard on the hard wood floor. It took a few seconds for, Angela to come back around. She slowly looked over to her right and saw, Roxy staring at her with her eyes wide open. It's seems as if Roxy landed awkwardly on her neck and broke her spine in the process. Angela rolled over and made it to one knee when she looked up and saw several guns pointed in her face.

"I'm glad you could join us Angela," the Lion said with a smile he nodded to one of his soldiers and the soldier quickly patted, Angela down and removed anything that she could use as a weapon.

The Lion kneeled down and handed Angela a bottle of water. "Here, looks like you could use this." Angela took the bottle of water and turned it up quickly guzzling the water. "Would you all excuse me for a second? I would like to have a word with, Ms. Angela," the Lion said as he Angela, and two of his soldiers stepped off into a room that was located at the end of the hall. "Please make yourself at home," the Lion sat on the edge of his desk. "So why are you trying so hard to capture me?" the Lion chuckled. "What's so special about me?"

"You kill innocent people and you're trying to attack America," Angela huffed.

"Not true!" the Lion said quickly. "What I'm doing is making sure that every country has the same opportunity. It's not fair that America gets to boss all the little people around if the little people don't do what America says then they get bombed, those days are over!" The Lion poured himself and drink and sipped it slowly. "I'm just simply standing up for the people who can't stand up for themselves."

"I'm going to enjoy killing you!" Angela growled.

"That's not a very nice thing to say," the Lion smiled. "In six months I'll be the most powerful man in the world as well as the richest and the only reason you're alive right now is because I want you on my team," the Lion took another slow sip from his drink. "With me and you on the same team we'll be unstoppable and I can make you a very rich woman."

"Fuck you!" Angela growled. "I'd never work with a scumbag like you. I'd rather die."

"Look at you Angela," the Lion gave her a sad look and shook his head. "You all bloody and battered for what? How much is your agency even

paying you? Huh? I bet your knees are killing you,"
he chuckled. "Come and work with me and you can
make your own rules, your own schedule, be your
own boss."

While, the Lion spoke, Angela looked around
the office to see what she could use as a weapon.

"Angela, let me help you," the Lion looked in
her eyes. "Me and you together and we'll be
unstoppable,"

Angela sprang from her chair and leaped
towards, the Lion, but he swiftly stepped to the side
and landed a stiff over hand right to, Angela's
temple that dropped her dead in her tracks. One of,
the Lion's soldiers hit, Angela in the back of her
head with his rifle knocking her unconscious.

"Stupid cunt!" the Lion bark. "Take her
downstairs to the basement and wait for me," he
order as he watched his soldiers do as they were
told.

TWENTY-7

STAYING ALIVE

Ashley made it to the second level of the mansion, snuck up behind a soldier, and slit his throat from ear to ear she then quietly dragged the dead soldier's body out of plain sight. Ashley continued on throughout the mansion when she heard the sound of feet shuffling behind her. Ashley spun around with her finger on the trigger ready to fire.

"Wait, don't shoot, it's me!" Troy said in a

strong whisper with his hands raised in the air.

"What the hell are you doing here and why are you creeping up on me like that?" Ashley fumed.

"I figured you two could use my help," Troy said with a smile. He quickly walked over to the soldier that, Ashley had just killed and began to remove the dead man's clothes. Minutes later, Troy stood up dressed in the dead soldier's uniform. "I'll go and see if I can find Angela."

Ashley reached out and grabbed, Troy's arm stopping him in mid stride. "If you get a clean shot of, the Lion, take it!" Troy nodded then continued on down the hallway. Ashley stood and watched as, Troy disappeared around the corner before she continued on in the opposite direction. Ashley moved along the shadows of the mansion and took out as many soldiers as she could one by one. It seemed like for every soldier that she killed another one popped up. Ashley moved in a low crouch over towards the rail, she looked down and saw a room full of people all standing around socializing and having a good time. Ashley grabbed a grenade from her utility belt, pulled the pin, and then tossed the grenade over her shoulder. The grenade landed in the middle of the crowd and before anyone could realize what had just happened it exploded.

BOOOOOOOM!

Ashley then quickly sprung from behind the rail and opened fire on the last remaining soldiers that stood around with lost and confused looks on their faces. Ashley dropped the last remaining soldiers with pinpoint accuracy. Ashley stepped over several dead bodies when she came across, Mary Wiggings trying to crawl her way towards safety; both of her legs were missing. Mary struggled as she pulled herself across the floor she couldn't believe how things went from good to horrible in a matter of seconds. Her crawl came to a stop when she saw a pair of combat boots blocking her path. Mary looked up and saw, Ashley staring down at her.

"Ashley please help me," she begged with no remorse. Ashley aimed her gun at the top of, Mary's head and squeezed the trigger several times. Ashley had a look of hatred on her face she looked as if she was thinking about spitting on, Mary's corpse. "I hope you burn in hell," Ashley snarled as she continued on throughout the mansion now all that was left for her to do was find, the Lion and kill him.

TWENTY-8

MAKE IT GO AWAY

When, Angela finally came back around, she found herself bound to a metal chair sitting in the middle of the room with several soldiers lined up against the wall.

The Lion turned around with a smile. "Ah, I see you finally decided to wake up. Perfect timing because I have a wonderful surprise for you," he announced as he began to slowly roll up his sleeves. "I gave you an easy way out, an opportunity to join me. But no you just had to do things the hard way," he paused as he picked up a needle and plucked the base of it. "Now you're going to see what happens when you go against, the Lion!"

Three soldiers entered the room with concerned looks on their faces. "Boss we have some trouble upstairs,"

"I'll take care of it in a second," the Lion said not bothering to turn and look at his soldiers. Angela looked up and prepared herself to be injected with whatever was inside of the needle when she spotted, Troy standing behind, the Lion wearing a soldier's uniform.

"I thought you were a smart woman," the Lion stood over, Angela looking down at her. "But it seems like you've been brainwashed by your government. The sad part about it is you're a great agent just on the wrong team." The Lion grabbed, Angela's arm and got ready to jam the needle in it when he heard a loud blast followed by a powerful force slam into the top of his shoulder. Not even a second passed before he felt another blast explode into the middle of his back forcing him to drop down to the floor and lose his grip on the needle. As, the Lion was falling down to the floor in the same motion he snatched one of his .45's from his holster and shot, Troy twice just as he hit the floor. The Lion then quickly opened a latch on the floor and disappeared down into a tunnel. Angela watched in horror as, Troy hit the floor and grabbed his mid-section she could tell that he was in excruciating pain from the look on his face. Angela knew that, Troy wasn't a field agent like her and, Ashley he was more on the tech side so to see him on the floor wincing in pain really bothered, Angela. Angela rocked her chair back and forth until the chair tipped over on its side she reached her hand out, grabbed a broken piece of glass, and began to slowly saw at the duct tape that bounded her wrist together. After a minute of sawing, Angela was finally able to free herself she quickly ran over to, Troy's aid and kneeled down with a worried and concerned look on her face. "How bad is it?"

"I'm good," Troy flashed a fake smile to let Angela know that he was okay. "I'm wearing a vest but one of the bullets must have went through," he nodded down towards the blood that seeped through his fingers. "I saved your life," Troy said with a satisfied look on his face. "I saved, the Teflon Queen's life."

"Yes you sure did," Angela grabbed Troy's gun from off the floor. "You wait right here I have to go stop, the Lion."

"You're better than him Angela you're the best!" Troy whispered. Angela nodded then jumped down into the tunnel and went after her target.

***

The Lion splashed threw several puddles of muddy water as he trotted through the dimly lit tunnel. He wasn't able to run at his full speed due to the two gunshot wounds he'd just suffered. Blood ran down his arm making his grip on the .45 a little slippery. The Lion ran until he couldn't run anymore. He looked over to his left and saw a steel ladder he quickly climbed up the ladder and moved the steel door that led above ground. The Lion pulled himself through the hole that led out to the back of the mansion; he quickly jogged through the snow. The Lion reached the woods when he peeked over his shoulder and saw, Angela not far behind. "Shit!" the Lion cursed as he ran through the woods, he reached down into his pocket and pulled out a cell, and he pressed one button and began speaking. "Yeah I'm coming your way now have the chopper ready to go!" he yelled, and then slipped the phone back down into his pocket.

TWENTY-9

NOT ON MY WATCH

Angela entered the woods and slowed down her pace. She was on full alert as her eyes scanned from left to right; she held a strong two-handed grip on her weapon as the snow crunched under her feet with each step that she took. Angela looked out into the darkness and didn't see, the Lion anywhere. Angela moved throughout the woods when two gunshots echoed loudly. Angela ducked down behind a tree. A big chunk of the tree shattered inches above her head. Angela darted out from behind the tree and fired off five shots before diving behind another tree. The Lion peeked from behind a huge rock and opened fire on, Angela as she ran for cover. The two took turns taking shots at one another until both of their guns were empty.

The Lion stepped from around the rock and tossed his gun down to the floor. "I know your gun is empty!" he yelled. "You might as well come on out so we can get this over with!"

Angela stepped from around the tree and tossed her empty gun down into the snow, then slowly made her way towards, the Lion.

"I gave you a chance to join the winning team," the Lion said. "Now I have to kill you."

"Or die trying," Angela took a fighting stance. The Lion charged at her hard throwing blows from all angles. Angela blocked and weaved a lot of the blows but several of them still managed to find a home on her face. Angela faked high and went low scooping, the Lion's legs from under him and dumping him down on his head in a pile of snow. Angela landed on top of, the Lion but he held a firm grip on Angela's neck and applied pressure.

"Arghh!" Angela growled as she managed to slip her head out of, the Lion's grip. She was rewarded with a swift kick to the face. The Lion quickly crawled back to his feet and took off in a sprint. He ran in a zigzag motion doing his best to lose, Angela but it was no use he looked behind him and there she was right there. The Lion came running out of the woods as if he was shot out of a cannon he reached the chopper and climbed his way on board when he felt a strong pair of hands grab him from behind pulling him off the helicopter. Angela and, the Lion landed hard on the pavement. Angela punched, the Lion in the mouth then tried to strangle him but, the Lion managed to slap her hands away, he landed several hard kicks to, Angela's chest and face all with the same leg. The

Lion threw another kick but, Angela caught his leg and swept his other foot from up under him. Angela held, the Lion's ankle in a two handed grip and gave it a sickening twist.

"Argghhh!" the Lion howled in pain as he heard his ankle snap. He reached down to his other ankle, pulled the back up .22 from his ankle holster, and tried to shoot, Angela in the face. Angela moved her head in the nick of time, the bullet exploded in her shoulder instead of in between her eyes.

"Argh!" Angela dropped down onto her back holding her bloody shoulder. The Lion limped to his feet and stood over, Angela with his gun trained at, Angela's head. "So long Teflon Queen!"

Angela shut her eyes and prepared herself for the last gun shot that she would ever hear.

POW!

Angela opened her eyes and saw, the Lion still standing over her the only difference was now he had a small bullet hole in the center of his forehead.

Angela watched as, the Lion's body landed face first down onto the pavement. Angela looked behind her and saw, Ashley standing there holding a smoking gun. Angela smiled as she laid on the pavement with her eyes shut and a smile on her face she was so thankful that this mission was finally over.

Ashley quickly hopped on the chopper and snatched the pilot out of the front seat by his neck. "It's finally over!" Ashley said in a victorious tone as she kneeled down by, Angela's side. "Look what I found," she held, the Lion's laptop in her hand with a huge smile plastered across her face. "This is all the evidence we need to clear our name,"

Angela smiled, "How's, Troy holding up?"

"He's fine I just called in for medical support."

"Thank you for saving my ass once again."

"I'm just glad this is finally all over!" Ashley laid down beside, Angela as the two waited for the medical team to arrive.

THIRTY

I'M OUT

Angela and, Ashley stood out front of the federal holding facility where they had been waiting for the past hour when finally, a door opened and, Captain Spiller was released. Captain Spiller walked out of the building with a smile on his face. "I knew you two would come through for me."

"I'm sure you had your doubts," Ashley said with a smile.

Captain Spiller grabbed both of the women and put them in a bear hug. "Thank you so much!"

"No thank you for trusting and believing in us," Angela smiled.

"Where's that cunt Mary Wiggings?"

"Dead!" Ashley answered quickly.

"Well I have to get back to the office I'm sure there's plenty of more work to do," Captain Spiller smiled.

"I'm out," Angela said with a straight face.

"I'm confused. What do you mean?" Captain Spiller asked not quite understanding what, Angela meant.

"I mean I'm out. I quit. I'm done," Angela spoke in a calm tone. "I'm off to live a regular life like normal people."

Captain Spiller laughed. "Even if we tried we'd never be able to live a normal life...ever!"

"Well I guess we'll have to see then won't we," Angela spoke in an even tone the look on her face serious. She turned and hugged, Ashley tightly. "I'm so proud of you, you have grown into a wonderful, beautiful woman, and I'll always be here for you if you need me," she smiled. "And make sure you look after, Troy he's a good man," and with that being said, Angela turned and walked off.

"Hey Angela!" Captain Spiller called out. "You'll be back!"

Angela winked at him. "Maybe."

TO BE CONTINUED

Click here to join our mailing list for new release updates

Or **Text Good2go to 42828 To Join!**

New Release

Business is Business PT 1,2,3 & 4 by Silk White

Now Available

To submit a manuscript for review, email us at

g2g@good2gopublishing.com

To order books, please fill out the order form below:

To order films please go to www.good2gofilms.com

Name:_____

Address:_____

City: _____ State: _____ Zip Code: _____

Phone:_____

Email:_____

Method of Payment: Check   VISA   MASTERCARD

Credit Card#:_____

Name as it appears on card: _____

Signature: _____

Item Name	Price	Qty	Amount
48 Hours to Die – Silk White	$14.99		
Business Is Business – Silk White	$14.99		
Business Is Business 2 – Silk White	$14.99		
Childhood Sweethearts – Jacob Spears	$14.99		
Flipping Numbers – Ernest Morris	$14.99		
Flipping Numbers 2 – Ernest Morris	$14.99		
He Loves Me, He Loves You Not - Mychea	$14.99		
He Loves Me, He Loves You Not 2 - Mychea	$14.99		
He Loves Me, He Loves You Not 3 - Mychea	$14.99		
He Loves Me, He Loves You Not 4 – Mychea	$14.99		
He Loves Me, He Loves You Not 5 – Mychea	$14.99		
Lost and Turned Out – Ernest Morris	$14.99		
Married To Da Streets – Silk White	$14.99		
My Besties – Asia Hill	$14.99		
My Besties 2 – Asia Hill	$14.99		
My Besties 3 – Asia Hill	$14.99		
My Boyfriend's Wife - Mychea	$14.99		
My Boyfriend's Wife 2 – Mychea	$14.99		
Never Be The Same – Silk White	$14.99		
Stranded – Silk White	$14.99		
Slumped – Jason Brent	$14.99		
Tears of a Hustler - Silk White	$14.99		
Tears of a Hustler 2 - Silk White	$14.99		
Tears of a Hustler 3 - Silk White	$14.99		
Tears of a Hustler 4- Silk White	$14.99		
Tears of a Hustler 5 – Silk White	$14.99		
Tears of a Hustler 6 – Silk White	$14.99		
The Panty Ripper - Reality Way	$14.99		
The Panty Ripper 3 – Reality Way	$14.99		

The Teflon Queen – Silk White	$14.99		
The Teflon Queen 2 – Silk White	$14.99		
The Teflon Queen 3 – Silk White	$14.99		
The Teflon Queen 4 – Silk White	$14.99		
The Teflon Queen 5 – Silk White	$14.99		
Time Is Money - Silk White	$14.99		
Young Goonz – Reality Way	$14.99		
Subtotal:			
Tax:			
Shipping (Free) U.S. Media Mail:			
Total:			

Make Checks Payable To:
Good2Go Publishing
7311 W Glass Lane,
Laveen, AZ 85339

055 877 493

CPSIA information can be obtained
at www.ICGtesting.com
Printed in the USA
LVOW04s1707210116
471731LV00008B/138/P